NO FANCY LIFE

Told with lyricism and a keen sense of the natural world...

John Grey, a middle-aged man, leaves an established career and moves with his wife to a farm high in the hills of Aberdeenshire, where a herd of suckler cows is to be their sole source of future income. His friends think he needs his head examined, but John is a Yorkshireman, stubborn as they come, and he is a quick learner. He and his wife Charlotte face many challenges, including extremes of weather, the isolated situation of the farm, the cussedness of animals and of people, and the strangeness and charm of the Doric tongue.

NO FANCY LIFE

NO FANCY LIFE

by

Charlotte Grey

Dales Large Print Books
Long Preston, North Yorkshire,
BD23 4ND, England.

British Library Cataloguing in Publication Data.

Grey, Charlotte
    No fancy life.

        A catalogue record of this book is
        available from the British Library

        ISBN   978-1-84262-592-7 pbk

First published in Great Britain in 2001 by The Book Guild Ltd.

Published in Large Print 2007 by arrangement with
Book Guild Publishing

Dales Large Print is an imprint of Library Magna Books Ltd.

Printed and bound in Great Britain by
T.J. (International) Ltd., Cornwall, PL28 8RW

CONTENTS

GLOSSARY

ava – at all
brak – broke
buckrake – a tractor implement for lifting.
buskit – dressed, adorned
cauldrife – cold
cleise – clothes
close – yard
court – cattle pen
cowped – overturned
Crusher – Petty Officer
div-ye – do you?
dochter – daughter
dreich – dreary
drill – row
fit – what; foot
fly-cup – quick drink
fower – four
fu' – full, drunk
Gean – the wild cherry
grieve – foreman
haik – hay-rack

ingang – entry
jeely-piece – jam and bread
kizzen – cousin
knacker-man – slaughterer
knout – cattle
loon – a boy, youth
mirk – darkness
neep – a turnip
on yir lane – on your own
pinch – crow-bar
puckle – small quantity
quine – a girl; a young woman
roup – auction
skean-dhu – small dagger
skep – container
snell – keen, sharp, severe
spik – speech, gossip
steading – farm building
sweigh – swinging bar (over an open fire)
takkin' the lift – patronizing
tink – a tinker
trauchled – wearied; overworked
whin – gorse bush; furze
windflower – wood anemone
windrow – row of turned hay
wratch – wretch
zotz– eliminate; kill

1

'We'll tak' a cup...'

It became clear to John Grey that what he did and more especially what he spent was watched by his neighbours, their wives and children, old grandmothers and probably even by their shaggy cows and household pets instead of as normally just by his wife. He was told of the talk before they arrived: 'Chap frae Lunnon bought Burnside, needs his heid looked at!'; 'Fowk frae the Sooth, wid hae plenty o' siller'; 'A gey fancy life they hid and gied it up fe yon wee bit fairm at the back o' beyont!' He had done his best to explain that he was Yorkshire born and bred, had never lived in London and was not, decidedly not, rich: but it did not matter, he was too busy to care what locals or anybody else thought, entirely absorbed by the new life; other people could go hang.

The year drew towards its end and Hogmanay was important, more celebrated than Christmas by most people in the

Howe, who were said to go from house to house taking bottles of whisky to exchange a dram or probably a few drams with friends or anybody who happened to cross their path. Charlotte did some baking 'just in case' but John did not expect any revellers to reach Burnside, the highest farm of all, nor did he wish to be late out of bed – both of them needed all the sleep they could get and more. He was content to leave socialising to the future; like so much else it was in the lap of the Gods. Meanwhile they could take him or leave him; when he was not working about the farm he was reading farming stuff, what he had to know about the calving of cows, studying the diagrams and photographs and learning what could go wrong. Especially that – there seemed to be a lot.

Friends in Yorkshire kept in touch but let him know he was an idiot giving up everything for the sake of a parcel of land and a few animals. 'You could have done more or less the same thing with a weekend cottage down here' they said. To her amusement Charlotte was seen as having to follow him whether she liked it or not, a bit like Ruth in the Bible. 'That's me!' she smirked. 'Knee-high amid the alien turnips...' John's smile was enigmatic: he was not a man for explanations.

Late afternoon on December 31st brought a young man from a distant farm where his family had lived for generations. Gilbert was a graduate but John did not hanker after any formal qualification: it was more subtle, something beyond measurement he envied, it was Gilbert as a boy learning because he was living it, knowledge seeping into his blood and his bones as the farm cycle repeated itself. When he said as much to Gilbert the answer was friendly.

'A man like you, you'll easy pick it up ... but if you need a hand anytime jest gie us a shout.' Being young he was inspired to add, 'Have ye nivver thocht we micht envy you – ye've a great place for the beasts, an' alsoo if I micht say it–' his brown eyes sparkled at Charlotte, 'sic a very fine wife...'

Late that night Charlotte switched on the television but the programmes had a sort of sham gaiety which did not appeal. By contrast, walking over to the steading it was a pleasure to see the cows, one or two nibbling at wisps of hay in the troughs, some deeply asleep, others wide-eyed, gently cudding, as if they waited for the year to turn. At midnight the far off church bells hardly made an impact on the silence around them: there was no need to kiss or break the wonderful calm by saying the usual things.

New Year's Day and the alarm bludgeoned them to come alive. Groans. Yawns. 'You stay, have a lie-in...' A noble offer because the first feed was difficult for one person to handle. 'Noooaaaahyamawake ... 'll both go.'

Not much later a couple of Michelin men left the house and rolled over to the steading. Some padding would be peeled off and left about as working warmed them up and the early temperature improved; that was one reason why they seemed to need a quantity of scarves and gloves and woolly hats although it was nice when a lost jerkin turned up in the middle of a load of turnips. 'Look John, my suede thingummy, I thought it was over here!'

The cows were good to see as the day began, stretching, blinking, heaving themselves from the deep straw to amble towards the troughs. A spreading awareness – heads lifted, ears twitching, eyes missing nothing. Lines formed, stout bodies pressing against each other and pushing lesser weights out. It was turnip time.

Mrs Beeton might have pointed out that

first you had to get your turnips. Not easy. There was a simple device, a 'scarifier' to be attached to the three-point linkage of a tractor which, driven up and down the drills, loosened the turnips from the soil ready to be pulled by hand. A special knife or 'huik' was used to slash away roots and foliage – that is, 'top and tail' – before loading into a cart. Several loads were taken at a time but if kept too long in store the quality of the feed deteriorated. John and Charlotte accepted the chore as a change from anything they had ever done before and Charlotte had her 'Tale of a Turnip' to tell.

Feeding was oddly complex: cows eat hay and obviously the finer the quality the better, but there are other things in a diet – specially manufactured 'cobs' for instance with all the minerals and vitamins imaginable – and again there is the turnip, juicy and delectable beyond human understanding, well worth a cow fight. They discovered that lifting the containers, a mere scrape of plastic upon the concrete floor, could produce a rising hysteria. To fend off anarchy they had to be quick, very very quick.

So John worked out a fairly effective routine, the key being readiness as Shakespeare knew well. All food to be laid out, the hay, the straw, minerals, turnips and bought-in cobs in a selected safe place. It did not do to underestimate the reach of a cow teetering on hind legs, a lesson learned from bales tumbled into the court, trampled and mostly wasted, the twine chewed and worse, swallowed.

Hay first, racks filled to overflowing, then speed – chop, chop: skeps up and contents poured one after the other at a rate of knots. As of one mind animals converge on the first neep to hit the trough, then fan-like open out as more and more rain down, the final emptying seeing them lined up as usual to bite and crunch away until the last lip-smacking shred has gone. Time for a breath, the rest easy enough, more hay to the racks, straw spread in the courts, water checked, a lot of tidying, then very carefully the cache must be assembled for next time, turnips not to be seen, heard or smelled. A perfect motto, 'Be prepared'. If you can get things right.

On that first morning of a brand-new year the earth was sparkling after an overnight frost. 'Important to check their water,' John said. After the cows were fed he had to walk up the brae to the sheep while Charlotte fed geese, hens, cats, wild birds and lastly got their own breakfast ready. As sometimes happened he was delayed because there was muck in one of the water troughs. 'You're a dirty bugger!' he accused the nearest cow who may or may not have committed the gaffe. It needed a lot of straw to clear the mess and going for a fresh bale he noticed Charlotte staring down at the winding road. She turned and saw him and shouted: 'Look! All those cars! Coming here!'

Land Rovers, two of them, a pick-up truck, an old, old Ford and a Volvo estate, headlights vying with the daylight. People spilled out when they reached the farm close, and only one or two had John or Charlotte ever seen before. 'Happy N'Year' they called and shifted bottles to free hands to shake. The young sheepdog barking and scampering, unable to cope; the gander hissing mightily before turning to lead his dames away; a bantam cockerel shrilling from the top of a gatepost and repeating the challenge for good measure jerked Charlotte into action. 'Do come inside!' she offered rather faintly, 'everyone!'

Much later she wrote in the farm diary:

To bed just after midnight prepared to forget the famed Hogmanay. Up as usual for the feed but hadn't finished when they arrived: Revellers with bottles. Whisky, rum, gin, vodka (a lot!), sherry, port, mixers. All lined up on the kitchen table. All we had to do was to find glasses. Admit to feeling flustered, John straight from the muck, me with straws in my hair. Hilarious! Toasted the N'Year many times. Breakfast rolls picked up on their way so we had bacon 'butties' with pots of tea. Men with John to check everything: women washing up (true situation in these parts?). More food when they came back, more tea and more of the hard stuff.

John noticed one of the men (who?) calmly reach for the milk jug – did he think it was water? – top up a half-full glass of whisky and drink! Ugh!

John, less than sober, has agreed to take on the coaching of a tug-of-war team. He knows nothing about T-O-W. So much for Hogmanay.

2

'Tale of a Turnip'

Charlotte's 'Tale of a Turnip' needs to be told because it illustrates what the new life might offer a woman who followed her man into the wilds: Ruth in the Bible comes to mind again though she went with her mother-in-law to good corn-growing country.

Out there among the drills it was warm work though the air they breathed was sharply cold. Looking at the sweep of farmland below and all around she felt good, primitive maybe but good, not a soul in sight: the only people in this world were John and herself.

In an old book John had found a reference to a man called Adolphus Speed who in the year 1659 praised turnips as excellent for feeding and fattening all sorts of cattle, saying that cows fed on them gave milk with 'full vessels' three times a day throughout the year. 'Nothing new under the sun!' John said when he passed this information on to

Charlotte as they sliced off most of the greenery before aiming each missile at the growing pile in the cart.

'Good old Adolph!' she agreed. 'So right in 1659!'

The clear air and timeless feel of it all made them lighthearted with a tendency towards silly jokes – 'Adam finding it cold pulling neeps and having the bare-faced cheek to ask Eve to help!' 'Michelin man and his not-so-spare spouse would cope better!'

But it could be different. Horizontal sleety rain an icy whiplash against the face, eyes blurred and stinging, accurate aim lost and neeps toppling into ever-deepening mud, slimy and disgusting to pick up for another shot. The loaded cart slewing and jerking over the rutted track getting totally bogged down at gateways where the soil was churned into a morass. Rain, hail, sleet or snow, it was no joke.

Once when John had to go to Aberdeen to sort out some muddle at the tax office, Charlotte took the tractor and cart to get at least one load of neeps before he returned. It was a cold, rough sort of day, the ground wet and everything more difficult, the threat of more rain to come causing her to hurry and make stupid errors in handling the

22

machine. Dusk had fallen as she made unsafe progress back to the steading, almost clipping a gatepost and making a lurching slide onto a slightly better surface beyond it. A bit heart-in-the-mouth she conceded, tipping the load into the shed. A little later the telephone rang in the house, and still towelling herself dry she answered cheerfully enough: it was so good to be back in the kitchen where three little cats quite indifferent to weather conditions were melted into the most comfortable chairs.

Joe Waddell, who might fairly be described as a dour kind of man, was telephoning to say he had witnessed the solo turnip-gathering and felt it necessary to warn: 'Ye shouldnae gang on yir lane fe neeps, nae wi' yon cairrt, nae sae late onywye. It's nae richt wark fe wifies!' Charlotte listened, tight-lipped. 'Ye micht hiv cowped the cairrt.' His voice was doom-laden, 'an' wha'd a kent i' sic mirk?'

She managed not to snap back at him, 'Why, you for one, you old...' or with heavy sarcasm suggest that John might have missed her, particularly if his supper was not waiting his return from the granite city. As evenly as she could she said politely, 'How kind of you to telephone, Mr Waddell. You see I did not realise how dark it was getting and it certainly is difficult getting the neeps after all the rain. The weather has been against us all lately, has it not? Thank you anyway, I promise to remember what you say!' He sounded almost cheerful as they exchanged goodbyes: it must have been enormous fun watching her struggle. Better still if the cart had 'cowped' to give him the joy of dialling 999 – or would he have bothered? She started to prepare supper seething with annoyance and more than ready to tell all.

On hearing the tale, John unexpectedly burst out laughing. 'Joe's right!' he said. 'Absolutely right! Only a bloody idiot would pull neeps in the dark!' He then moved like lightning through the kitchen door and upstairs to change from his decent city suit.

3

'Noo that cauldrife winter's here...'

Speaking to John and Charlotte people used words like 'dreich', 'snell' and 'cauldrife'; soft Scottish voices lingered over these words and a wry frown or a shake of the head would imply that Burnside was no place to be except in spring or summer, 'When the bonny days are come,' as one man said without knowing he was a poet. It was plain that they should prepare for a siege; Charlotte wondered if she had been right to turn the large pantry into a shower-room but dismissed the thought. 'Survival' might be the key word but a good sluice after sweaty work was a boon; they could store tinned food anywhere, even in the loft. It was hard to imagine popping up there for a tin of beans, but still...

In early January temperatures plummeted sharply, then eased. They awoke to a strange diffusion of light on the ceiling of their bedroom and drew back the curtains to a silent world. No longer was Lochnagar's cap of snow unique; hills, fields and farms shared a dazzling white blanket, and the rising sun touched all with gold. It was breathtaking. Charlotte tried to imagine a Scottish word to describe it.

It took a long time to dig themselves out of the house and towards the steading. To their relief all was calm there, animals lying in deep straw, untroubled, cudding away.

'Wise of them, taking a lie-in,' said John.

'What's that?' Charlotte queried. She felt good: red in the face, perspiring or down-right sweaty, nevertheless it was great to have coped so far. 'Cauldrife winter at last!' she called over to John as he leaned over docile Lucy, their model cow, to check the water in one of the troughs, 'and we get them fed as usual.'

Cattle courts had to have a good circulation of air to keep the animals in good health and snow had come in through every opening designed for this: deep in places it meant more hard digging and finding somewhere away from any bedding area for disposal of it, but that was a problem for later, checking the sheep was more important. No need to feel worried about the hens who had a store of food inside their hut. The geese roamed free and would have found shelter but Charlotte collected an amount of corn, being unable to face the gander's fierce eye without bearing gifts for him and his ladies.

'Give it to me,' John said, reaching for the corn. 'I'll scout round the old buildings while you get us something to eat. We'll top up before tackling the hill which might be some job!' Charlotte was most surprised – they never fed themselves until every animal was dealt with but she went back along the narrow path they had dug from the house. How docile she had become as a 'fairmer's wife', on the surface anyhow: independence seemed a scarce sort of flower in the hills. She lifted the shiny Aga lids and took bacon, sausages and tomatoes from the fridge. They would have the lot, even fried bread which normally she considered a health hazard: forcing a way through the drifts would dissipate excess calories.

John kept what he called his 'embryo flock' on the rough higher ground a good way from the house and buildings. He intended to take drastic steps to clear and improve this area; in the meantime a few hardy ewes found grass enough to keep them going, with mineral blocks as a supplement and 'a puckle hay' as Gilbert advised when the weather was really bad. Cleared and improved, the ground would support them and their offspring as time went on. At the far edge of his land a small copse of Scots pine trees, sparse of foliage, stunted and bent by storm winds, just about survived the challenge of encroaching scrub. Bleached stumps and gnarled roots told of a more substantial forest in days gone by. Having repaired and built up dykes bordering the copse, John hoped to find the ewes there – the gorse might break the depth of snow; it was a likely place, instinct should lead them to such a haven.

All paths had disappeared. Slow and tentative, probing with tall sticks and much relieved when the probes met nothing, they reached the copse and the sheep were there, marooned but safe, clustering within the stout old walls, dumb, enduring, not buried as John had feared. With a great deal of effort he brought them more than a puckle of hay. The untidy scrub had served a useful purpose.

'When I do the clearing I'll be leaving a lot more than I thought. It shows you not to think like a suburban gardener wanting everything neat and tidy.'

'Shelter,' Charlotte agreed. 'Shelter, all-important.' As a little girl she remembered praying for 'Shelter for man and beast.'

The light was perfect and Charlotte took several photographs intending them for the farm diary with a caption something like, 'The sheep which were lost and then found'. Unaware that she too might figure in the diary, Charlotte stopped for a moment on the way back, spellbound by the expanse of sparkling white, untouched except by their own feet or the small tracks of rabbit or hare. John quickly took a photograph, Charlotte's stance penguin-like, arms pushed out by the thick padding of her coat; an uplifted face, smiling. In the diary the caption could read: 'As I walked through the wilderness of this world'. That day it was easy to feel like 'Pilgrim'.

The weather showed little change. In the Howe roads were cleared and life more or less returned to normal but long farm tracks remained blocked and the hill farmers dug deep into stores and had to bide their time.

John Grey tried not to think about cost as he substituted bought-in sugar beet nuts for the neeps he could not get at. With the tractor out of action some routine tasks could not be done and others tackled by hand took up much more time. Charlotte found time to bake bread in the Aga and the loaves turned out brown and wholesome, the kitchen redolent of other days, old-fashioned and nice.

'That is really tasty!' John said as he crammed the last of one slice into his mouth and reached for another. 'I'm a pig, but you've excelled yourself this time, better than cake in my opinion. You've got yourself a job for life!'

'Well, who knows?' She was torn between being delighted and not wanting all the loaves to disappear like snow in summer. 'Anyhow, it's the Aga not me, it just seems to bake it right whatever I do.' She blessed the day they had bought the range at a price inflated beyond all expectation. John had agreed only because he could tell she wanted it. That was before money became so tight. But it was worth its weight in gold and made the kitchen the best place in the house for warmth and comfort, especially now when they were truly on their own.

'And modest with it!' John gave her a playful slap as he lifted another slice. 'It's all right, I'm off, but I do need to stoke up, you know that. How long have I got? An hour, two?' It amazed her that he could be thinking of the next meal and supposed that she was doing the right thing preparing what he sometimes called 'big eats'. At the same time she felt guilty for being inside where it was warm and doing something so easy and pleasant. Outside work was hard and exhausting, yet afterwards you felt elated, pleased with yourself, cock-a-hoop in spite of being worn out.

Earlier she had casseroled rabbit and now she placed the best pieces, the boned back and legs, into a deep pie-dish and after putting a funnel into the centre began to make pastry. She tried not to think of John shooting the rabbits and also her cats had to be ignored, one scratching at the kitchen door, another pawing at the window. Rabbit, self-caught or cooked, was their dream food: no surprise they had sussed it out. Later they would be given the meat off the front legs but meantime were banished – she was unfailingly careful about hygiene. While the pastry rested she chopped leeks and sliced one or two parboiled potatoes, packing them round the rabbit, and then added stock from the casserole. Just the secret ingredient to add she thought, smiling to herself and reaching into the cupboard for a tin. No one, no one ever would prize this secret from her: it was from France, originally given to her grandmother on condition she did not tell all and sundry. It made her feel clever, knowing one of the tricks of French cuisine, though basic common-sense told her that the best French chefs would not touch rabbit. She had not dared put this to grandmama.

She cut out pastry to fit the dish and made a nicely indented edge: she could not resist cutting out pastry leaves to decorate, bending and curving them, arranging them in an artistic pattern round the centre. Thoughtfully she added a rosette there before brushing the whole with beaten egg. She checked the time before putting it into the Aga.

Their snowbound world and its silence had become so normal that a thunderous knocking on the door caused her to jump almost out of her skin. Then a shout from John: 'Go in, go on in!' and into the house came two men, Alastair and Abby, red-faced and perspiring, putting down sacks and boxes, stepping out of wellington boots, beaming at her and John who'd followed them. 'Och, we thocht ye micht be deid!' 'Starved! Supplies run out!' 'We're the mountain rescue!' They produced a bottle of Scotch. 'Nicked this from a St Bernard on the way up!' Explanations came thick and fast. Charlotte and John could not take it in, Alastair and his neighbour making this trip, sheer slog from where they had to leave the car, through deep drifts to the farm road and then uphill all the way carrying such a load. 'It makes me very annoyed to find ye're nae starving John, but ye'll get a dram for a' that!'

They sat at the long table and Charlotte produced the rabbit pie, its embellished crust browned perfectly, giving out a wonderful smell. 'Food for the gods!' said John, and the Sherpas agreed. Before they left on the long trek back to their car John got them to pose for a photograph with the load of supplies including 'the heaviest tatties in Aberdeenshire', Abby said, though Alastair claimed to have carried them most of the way. In the diary the picture looked like an attempt on Everest and its caption read: 'Alastair and Abby came to tea'.

Weeks later when the postie delivered mail again there was a letter from Charlotte's friend Lisa, written and posted when they were 'snowed-in'. The letter read:

I don't know how long this will take to reach you poor darlings – abandoned up there in the snowy wastes. I felt I had to write because you are being remembered and talked about down here in the civilised world, for instance at Mary's last night, their anniversary (entre nous she told me there was nothing, absolutely nothing to celebrate!).

We talked to several people who asked about you and shudder when they see your weather on the TV. Opinion is mixed: some say that John really has flipped and you will be fed up. I told them, 'No! it is a sort of Shangri-La and you love it.' Hope this is true.

Victor sends you his special love Charlotte. I believe he would fancy his chances if you get tired of S-L. He is as dishy as ever – super suits and smouldering eyes. Remember?

Saw Arthur Graham-Harvey last week, his book giving trouble – seems to have writer's block about a scene in Guatemala or was it Glasgow? Still has that pale and interesting look. Martha spending the earth on clothes, all designer labels and best cashmere, her winter boots the palest pink suede! How does he afford it?

Must cut this short as I have to get a meal – lots of packets to undo! Keep as warm as you can and let me have a word when the snow melts and you are free. Much love...'

They laughed, as intended. John was intrigued picturing Charlotte's admirer struggling up through the drifts, a sack of Aberdeenshire 'tatties' heavy against his splendid suit. 'His warm eyes would come in handy,' suggested Charlotte.

'Against hypothermia,' agreed John. Pale, interesting, Arthur would be blocked again and never make it through the snow, they decided, but Martha in finest cashmere and the pink boots just might.

4

'Parturio – *I bring forth...*'

When there seemed to be a slight thaw, John did what he could to clear the deep snow. The light tractor with a buckrake attached was painfully inadequate for the job. The farm required a bottomless purse: you had to get the priorities right and he, dammit, had not. He would have to rethink – a snow-plough for next year and something a lot more powerful than the handy little Zetor to operate it. Tidying behind the tractor his wife was becoming a dab hand with a shovel. When a good wide path was opened up he put the Zetor under cover and went back to take the heavy tool from her. The air seemed sharper. He saw Charlotte fasten the top button of her coat against the chill.

By next morning the cleared path was an ice-rink and every patch of melted snow a hazard. For the first time pipes in the cattle court froze and cows used to drinking gallons every day pressed around the trough

36

and bellowed. Closing his ears to it John un-did lagging and poured kettles of boiling water over the pipes with no result at all except a squelchy mess. Then inspiration! Charlotte's hair-dryer! Hot air applied to every inch of pipe produced seepage which incredibly the animals heard and understood before it formed a trickle. They were drawn towards the trough but here the 'survival of the fittest' notion was confirmed. Gertie, the boss cow got the first drops on her tongue and drank deeply when true flow came. Unchallenged, she lingered, lifting her head, savouring the icy liquid as it eased down her throat. She moved on only when the number two cow felt bold enough to give a nudge. All became quieter as in turn they drank, in the rightful order determined during their first days on the farm.

John, carefully replacing wadding round the pipes, gave thought to this evidence of a 'bunt', a similar thing to the 'pecking' order in hens. In any new herd of cows there will be aggressiveness or actual fighting until a social pattern is established, then all becomes calm, the top animal does not have to fight any more, the second one is sub-missive only to the 'boss' and so on. Gertie's residual horn was a key factor: John saw it as a boat's prow cutting a swathe through a tumbling sea of cows to capture the last turnip or a few sugar beet nuts. At first he had tried to improve the lot of those at the bottom of the scale, but it caused trouble, their 'betters' ready to clarify swiftly and unpleasantly the exact meaning of 'tail-ender'. So he learned to offer no favours, no handout unless it could be given with great subtlety. He had come to believe there was some simple animal equivalent of peace of mind and made it an aim to minimise stress in his herd. Both he and Charlotte were quiet amongst them. Good accommodation they had, probably the best around; dry bedding and more than adequate rations he had managed so far; all handling was as skilful as he could make it but any answer to Gertie's brutal horn was beyond him.

Hoping the coffee pot would be blipping on the stove he left the steading to report 'Everything flows': the muck-stained hair-dryer he placed in the toolbox in case it was needed again, by the cows.

Going over late that night to check the water and take his routine look at the animals before turning in, John met an almost horizontal bitter wind, sleet stinging viciously at his face and eyes, making him gasp after the warmth of the house. He walked round, registering in his mind how each cow looked, most of them cudding placid heaps in the well-bedded court, yet he felt uneasy. He counted, then a second time to confirm the number was one short.

He blundered over the ice to Charlotte who was half-asleep in her armchair. 'Get your coat and come – one of 'em's missing. Wrap up well!' They were soon in the steading, the cows stirring at the unaccustomed appearance of both so late. 'I'd better check.' There was no mistake but she could tell him, 'Anna, I can't see her! Number 83, She's the one!'

The path to the hill was hardly visible, a torch awkward to hold, its beam deflected by strong gusts. Blizzard, fiercer as they climbed, sleet thick on them, unmelting, finding a mark at wrists and throat; the effort a nightmare with no certainty that the cow was on the hill. Clambering, slipping, sprawling over iron-hard ground, breath choked back into lungs by shrieking demon winds, somehow they went on. Beyond all reason. They had to find Anna.

In a sense she found them because hearing their approach she gave a low moan, guiding them to where she had pushed a way into a clump of strangling whins. And there was no doubt, on this unholiest of nights, that Anna was trying to give birth.

'We'll have to get her home!' The words were wrenched from John's throat. He did not tell Charlotte what the wavering light from the torch had shown: from Anna's back end projected not a hoof or feet as would be normal, but a tail, which was not. Charlotte moved to the cow's head, closing in so the beast backed as they wanted but then for desperate moments staggered up-hill and further from sanctuary. Against all odds John got ahead and managed to turn her. Nothing now but the need to get down, to be shielded from the rage on the hill, to breathe and see and think...

They forced her slipping and stumbling dangerously but downwards, protesting and fearful, with piteous little moans, down towards cover and the help they hoped to give. It was ironic that their first calving should be this one.

With lower ground ahead the cow speeded up, quite outstripping their pace, forcing them to follow where she chose to go. Luckily she went along a narrow passage behind the main building and into one of the old cart sheds where she stopped, wild-eyed and trembling but safe. It remained only to secure her. John dragged a heavy gate to block off the open side, not easy but he found strength. Spreading a bale of straw, Charlotte realised her legs were jelly and she was trembling like Anna.

John, grim-faced, was pulling off his coat and rolling up his sleeves. 'Get the bag Charlotte, and the book.' He glanced at the dimmish light. 'And a better lamp and my glasses if you can.' She hurried to the gate on the close and cried out because it would not open: the bolt had iced up since they went through, hours ago it seemed. She had to climb over, bare hands sticking to frosted metal: she half fell to the road but, managing to keep on her feet, staggered to the house to collect what John wanted, the 'medical' bag and book, a lamp from the topmost shelf in a kitchen cupboard, his glasses left somewhere ... oh God, where?

Clumsy with all she carried, back over the gate to John soothing the cow, stroking, petting, trying to calm her. Specs on. The book opened at a fairly clear diagram. Antiseptic gel on hand and arm, then inside ... to confirm what an intermittent appearance of the pathetic dab of a tail had signalled: the calf was the wrong way round,

41

posterior first, and could well suffocate.

Hurry! hurry! the need pounding in his head but he had to make sure he got it right. The book again, held by Charlotte. Inside the cow a slow and steady push to move the calf further back so he could gently straighten out the hind legs, making birth possible. All now depended on how long she had struggled to expel it when all straining was in vain, how exhausted she might be, and whether it was too late anyway, the calf dead or dying.

They waited, expert help two or three miles away, as useless as if at the other side of the globe. How long since they started searching? How long before that had she been trying? There was no telling.

Lack of experience was a bitter taste in the mouth. All they really knew was cold and wet and being exhausted. Anna was motion-less, glassy-eyed, patently in a world beyond them. For the first time Charlotte faced the possibility that the cow might die, victim as they all were of a winter which would never end...

Confounding despair Anna suddenly gave a massive strain and then another, and like a cork from a bottle a long slithery creature was on the straw, twitching, choking, snuffling, most definitely alive. As if demented the cow warned John to keep away when he bent to clear the calf's nose and mouth of mucus: Anna was fiercely protective, totally taken over by instinct. Strangled moans came from her. She was tender and rough at the same time, frantically nuzzling and pushing the calf, licking away and swallowing all betraying birth fluids. They saw it was a bull calf.

Later, trying to thaw over the Aga, Charlotte said: 'Do you remember in the other vet book, the big green one, what it said?' She could not resist reaching for the book and finding the relevant page. 'Here, look.' In a solemn voice she read: '"Parturition (*parturio* – I bring forth) is more likely to proceed successfully without than with human assistance".'

'Is that so?' said John, picturing the diagram and his wife trying to hold it still under a swaying light. He poured generous amounts of 'the water of life' into two glasses. 'We can drink to that!'

Later in the year when the hill blazed with gold and wild flowers made a bonny patchwork along its paths, when grass in the fields was plentiful and the breezes were mild as milk, John photographed all his cows and calves for the farm record. When it was Anna's turn Charlotte hugged the sturdy calf, the mother keeping close watch.

'Label this one "Special" John.'

'Yes! The only one to come "erse fust".' He liked the local way of putting it.

5

'For the rain it raineth...'

Eventually they talked with Gilbert about the birth of the calf; what it had been like on the hill that awful night, seeing the tail, the fear of doing the wrong thing and afterwards the relief – homework, studying, the bag packed ready, all proved worthwhile.

Charlotte decided to be honest. 'I remember you were amused when you saw our books, and the calving bag packed – you thought that very funny!' she accused.

'Och, nae really, it was, well ... the only thing ye seemed to expect was disaster! It's nae like that, some of 'em pop oot easy, like shellin' peas, I'm tellin' ye, honestly!' It was no good, she was not in the mood, mouth set, brows in a frown.

'Oh come on, Charlotte, it wasn't Gilbert's fault the bloody thing was the wrong way round, or the rotten blizzard!' John knew at once he should have bitten the words back and tried a different tone. 'How about some coffee my duck? Is there any, love?'

There was a short answer: 'If you get it yourself!' She went upstairs away from both of them. It was cold and the room felt damp. She tried to see through rain-blurred panes; dark clouds hiding Lochnagar, the slopes striate, brown earth and thin departing snow. Rain, rain, rain. No more the shining, unblemished expanse to make you stop in wonder no matter what you were about. Climbing the hill with food for sheep or working on the paths or through the steading doors you would catch a glimpse of sun flooding everything with gold or crimson at the ending of the day.

Ordinary routine had gone, the light tractor was useless again: paths were streams, all else quagmire. At night the Aga was festooned with drying clothes, wet seeped through 'guaranteed waterproof'; wellington boots, damp and smelly, never quite dried out. Worst of all was the blockage of cattle-court drains, deeply-strawed comfort turned into squelching morass by invading water. The cows were refugees, huddling at the dryest end, the 'bunt' in operation.

They did their best, both working doggedly to free drains which almost immediately choked up again. Straw was a worry: how could they have used it so lavishly in fairly decent weather? Stocks were diminishing at a rate of knots. They discussed only day-to-day matters, plans for the future were best avoided; the past became a foreign land frighteningly preferable to the present thankless slog. Both were exhausted, stalked by depression. Looking at the bleakness of his wife's face and knowing it mirrored his own, John made attempts at humour but the words were lead balloons. Clearly there was nothing to smile about. Except Anna's calf.

Swathed in 'waterproofs', Charlotte took to paying frequent visits to Anna and the calf. It was vital to keep them healthy so Anna was given extra hay and nuts, and straw garnered from every nook and cranny. They dared not put her back with the herd because conditions in the court were not right for the calf. He was flourishing, a pleasure to look at, mainly dark red in colour with just a streak of white along the nose and a white splash above each shining little hoof. He was kept immaculate, Anna's tongue always at work on him. He would lift up his head as she reached under the chin, luxuriating, his long-lashed eyes blinking, his mouth opening slightly to show new pink gums.

Came the day when he squeezed through

the makeshift cart-shed gate, using the smallest of gaps to insinuate his lean body through to the outside world. John rushed out when he heard frenzied bellowing from the cow as her jewel sniffed and poked and splashed away from her. It took only minutes to return him, but Anna's fiercest licking could not quite restore the pristine nature of those elegant little feet which had strayed into the reality of mud.

Of course the rains stopped, but then came great gales as a scourge to the soaked earth. Solid objects were wrenched up to fall oddly; weightless like confetti, spinning, bounding, fluttering debris; the sky in chaos. Roofs gaped where heavy corrugated sheets had gone, transformed as magic carpets up and away on the swirling air. John called Charlotte to see two plump packages curveting over the steading until their swooping, soaring dance came to a final bow, one dipping, then seconds later the other. It was exhilarating to run down the farm road to find them, only just on Burnside land, snagged on what everybody called a 'piky wire' fence.

Charlotte was first and stood looking at pillows in polythene wrappers, brand-new, undamaged. John, a poor second in heavy wellington boots came panting alongside.

'They must have been left on somebody's doorstep – some clot of a delivery man who had never heard the weather forecast.' Knowing his wife's usual attitude, John added, 'I don't know how the heck we'll find out who they belong to or where they came from ... there's no ticket ... but I suppose you'll want to try.'

In fact Charlotte was only half-listening. She was thinking about Sister Maria Carmel at her convent school; large, with abundant fair hair and a sunny nature tolerant of small misdemeanours, unlike most of the nuns. One day walking two by two sedately through the park on the way back to school, Charlotte had seen a coin shining on the gravel and picked it up, hesitant, wondering if it was wrong. She had stolen a glance at Sister Maria who unbelievably was laughing.

'Go on there, Charlotte dear it's yours! Take it as a gift.' Back in the present the wind tugged at the parcels held close to her chest. Her smile was triumphant.

'Wrong my lad, not for the first time. No matter who they belong to, or where they came from, I believe they're mine now. And I'm taking them, as a gift from God!'

Suddenly on the hill a profusion of wind-flowers imitated the lost snow and spring touched Lochnagar with pale sunshine. There was some sort of legend about the mountain; if the snow ever vanished from its summit, dire things would come to pass in Scotland, or even further afield, depending on how pessimistic you were.

'It looks as if we might survive!' The snowcap gleamed white but John's words encompassed more than mere legend.

He decided to open all doors to the courts so the cows could go on the hill, and this they did at a rush; ladies great with child able to search for fresh green which showed first beneath gorse and whin bushes; to climb familiar slopes and rest there with space around and the wide sky above. Freedom was the name for it.

In the courts both worked to make things decent again, shovelling the wettest muck into the cart, dumping the loads in a great pile to rot down for use in the future. It was heavy, sweaty work but a relief after all the helpless waiting while problems mounted in never-ending rain.

'Hard work never hurt anybody, they say!'

Charlotte had to lean on the muck-fork, breathing fast, sweat trickling down her face. 'I reckon they say it,' she panted, 'because they've never tried it! Agree?'

They had to keep at it but when the cows, redolent with the peaty smell of the hill, came back to feed the court was dry and well-strawed.

'Like old times, girls! Or nearly,' a grimy, sweating John told them. 'Even if we're just about knackered!'

Charlotte had gone across earlier and now he left, looking forward to the casserole which been cooking in the Aga as they toiled away at the muck. He intended to have a good dram first, a custom some Scots seemed to favour and this day he could see why.

Zipping off soiled plastic coveralls before showering he thought of the men farming Burnside before him: how in hell had they coped he wondered? Lacking machinery and extra help, short of money as he undoubtedly was, yet he had so much to be thankful for – comfortable living, good stock, even the efficient little Zetor when it was not asked to work beyond its capacity. And they had so little, those people way back. Plenty of hands maybe, but how did they manage? Nothing to help them keep dry for instance, no wellingtons, no plastics. nothing easy. Fewer animals and a struggle to keep them healthy. And if you went further back still, what about old Adolph? Adolphus Speed, turnip man in the year 1659. If only he had the time to read more; he felt he owed it to them to learn more.

The casserole of beef was thick and tasty and Charlotte had added dumplings as a treat. John saw her face was pale and her eyes dark with fatigue but she was neat and clean as if she had never bundled herself into coveralls too big for her and slaved away at the great mass of muck. It was a job to make a strong man quail, as he well knew.

'Charlotte,' he said, 'that wasn't a bad day's work for a rich man's lady wife!'

The next morning a cow was missing at first count. They found Gertie far up on the hill near a stone dyke well sheltered by spreading junipers. A burn in spate further protected her. It was a good, well-chosen place and beside the cow was a small fat replica of herself. Was it just imagination that its face seemed belligerent? There was no sign of trauma, all so peaceful that Charlotte had to admit it must've been a normal birth.

A photograph taken for the diary showed an alert cow daring them to come near. It was entitled 'Gertie, the boss cow and a shelled pea'.

6

'What pain it was to drown...'

The hill was the place for calving. John and Charlotte learned a lot – where the chosen place was likely to be in the lee of a dyke or a thick clump of gorse, somewhere close to a stream. A cow would make her way outside, to be quite alone, neither cows nor humans near. Gilbert warned them about this.

'If ye see one fairing to calve don't whativver ye do get too close or she'll likely move off, jis' when she should not. It's better tae keep yir distance; let her git on with it!' A sly look at Charlotte. 'An' when the time comes ye can dive in! If ye wish.'

'At the ready!' John agreed.

The signs of 'fairing to calve' were mentioned in all the reading matter and they began to see them, little things that added up if you were alert. They noticed a cow might go off up the hill but return to feed in the building as usual before resuming her lonely vigil outside. So in effect there was a walk up and down for nothing but they could not afford to leave anything to chance. Often they had this unnecessary sort of trip, and waited about endlessly in the cold, and in the dark sometimes, because they dared not take the risk of misjudging the moment of birth. However, late or early, one of them was likely to be watching, anxious, relieved, ever conscious of a miracle lifting the spirit beyond tiredness. Once in a while, and it was a very pleasant thing, a cow would be found with a calf tucked well down beside her already suckled and content, the mother peaceful, cudding. It was a marvel to see a newly-born calf staggering on spindle legs, falling, recovering, eventually nudged to the udder, finding, losing the teat, finding it again and then life-giving suckling and a tail shimmying joy! Easy once you got the knack!

There was an abundance of mothering instinct on Burnside hill: it had to be judged as superior to that of a good many human beings.

'Some people could learn a lot from these dumb animals,' Charlotte was certain, 'some of those you read about in the tabloids.' John tried to think of his last sight of that kind of paper and remembered it as about a year ago or even longer, squinting over somebody's shoulder in an Aberdeen bus. It could have been the *Sun* which he would never buy, or maybe the *Daily Record*, another one outside his range. Or Charlotte's come to that.

'Yeah!' he agreed absently, looking down at their latest acquisition. 'Four legs good, two legs bad!'

It was Lucy who had produced the calf, Lucy his idea of a model cow and naturally it had been a copybook birth. After Lucy a cow they named Suzy had twins, not so unusual in itself, but what followed proved traumatic, a real test of endurance for man, woman and beast. It began when Charlotte on an early morning round could not find Suzy: the cow seemed to have disappeared. She was not in the court, or on the hill or in any known place. It became bewildering and time-consuming, there was nowhere... Charlotte sat down to think, trying to resist an impulse to go a second time over the same ground – after all, you could hardly miss something as big as a cow, and Suzy was huge, one of the largest. Several parks adjoined the hill and had gates – it was just possible? She went to check and the second gate was slightly ajar, its chain hanging loose. Trudging down the slope she disturbed a hare which shot off at a tangent and then came to a stop on reaching a wall, blending into the stones, motionless, posed as invisible.

The burn at the foot of the slope was in spate and across it on a small plateau left by the curve of the stream as it flowed away from their land, there was Suzy. Against the strong thrust of water she had reached the little sheltered oasis, and had given birth, but she seemed to be alone – there was no sign of a calf. Trying to reach the cow without getting too wet Charlotte moved downstream a little way and to her horror saw a small black thing in the water, bobbing up and down. Worse, further along still, buffeted against the bank, another tiny bit of flotsam... Both were incredibly heavy. It took all Charlotte's strength to drag them onto the bank where they lay like dead seals, water trickling ice-cold from sleek black coats, jaws clamped as if one solid piece, no visible eyes. From across the burn the cow watched.

Against all reason Charlotte began to rub fiercely at the bigger bundle. Hopeless it had to be, yet her whole being rebelled against the terrible waste of life, the pain and helplessness of the cow. She kept on, pounding roughly at the little dead thing, gasping and sobbing in frustration, knowing herself to be a fool for trying and then ... oh please God, was that a slight tremor, very faint? She did not know whether she had imagined it and carried on not daring to hope. It was exhausting and she needed help but could not leave. Would John wonder where she had got to and start looking?

She saw him coming down the brae. 'Get straw,' she yelled, 'as much as you can!' If only this calf could be revived and put onto the cow. Otherwise, with her udder bursting with milk, they had problems. There was definite movement now and massage was easier using a wedge of the straw. Together they lifted both calves onto heaps of it and John was surprised at the weight. 'Must have taken muscle Charlotte?'

'Wonder-woman!' she agreed, and allowed him to take over for a few minutes, to concentrate on the bigger calf seemed best. At increasing signs of life John decided to fetch Suzy; if she would do her stuff...

It proved difficult. She was disinclined to move, showing fear of the swiftly flowing water: she looked numbed and dejected after the ordeal of birth and loss. John had to shout and smack her across the back to force her and it alarmed him to see how she stumbled and almost collapsed onto the straw beside the calves. For her sake he pulled the live calf close and then, with a flash of inspiration, lifted its head to the swollen udder, prizing open frozen jaws and clamping them round a teat. Miracle of miracles when after a second it began feebly and then more strongly to suck.

Tears streamed down Charlotte's face as she rubbed with renewed vigour at the second twin. This one seemed even more hopeless, but it had worked before. She was becoming very tired, her arms and neck painful beyond words, her hands losing grip, fingers scraped raw. It seemed a very long time since she found Suzy.

John had gone to get food, the best hay he could muster, and a couple of chopped turnips, blessed turnips now nearly all gone. Usually, concentrates were not fed to a newly-calved animal but he brought some for Suzy because her need was great. She ate avidly and began to look better. He made several trips with more hay and straw bales to pack round the little group for shelter and then had to leave because he saw another cow was giving birth. Charlotte worked on. The little trembling sign of life came, almost imperceptible this time, but giving hope. Suzy slowly stood to pass a massive afterbirth and settled down again. Later Charlotte was able to put the second calf to her and blessedly it too managed to suck. More than six hours had passed.

How much earlier were the twin calves born? John at midnight had seen no sign. When and how did both calves end up in the burn? How long were they slowly drowning there? Questions never to be answered.

John telephoned the vet because the second twin could not stand properly, though it made an attempt at walking with front feet bent at the knuckles, 'knuckled under' in fact. This seemed the only visible defect in either calf. The vet was quite breezy. 'Contracted tendons! Quite common, will right itself!'

Gradually Suzy improved. Towards the evening she was on her feet grazing though not going far from the two black bundles. Early the following morning she was half-way up the slope, standing to suckle a calf on each side, one still on its knuckles. Next day found her at the gate looking to the herd as it grazed around the hill; two very well-polished little bulls stood four-square beside her.

Charlotte's hands and forearms were painfully swollen but she felt extremely pleased with herself. She imagined only someone like Grace Darling rescuing a whole boat's crew could have felt better.

When they got round to a write-up for the diary it was unusual to find the twins together when the light was right for a photograph. At dusk, like all other calves, they joined in a grand run, hurtling at speed round the perimeter of the field. Often a new mother would follow in the wake of the runners in a swaying despairing trot, bellowing for her particular calf to come back, which it never did – galloping was too much fun. John discovered from the green book that this grand gallop was an important part of the process of maturing, causing the juices to flow, helping digestion and growth. It was also riotously funny to watch.

When they got a photograph of the three together the caption Charlotte wanted did not make much sense until the whole story was told. It read: 'Flotsam twice: the Water Babies with Suzy'.

7

'Gather ye rosebuds...'

Given by a former laird in memory of sons killed in the First World War the hall, built of granite to his specifications, contained one fair-sized room floored in oak and half-lined in varnished pitch pine for concerts and dances. There was a smaller room for meetings, a kitchen, cloakrooms and lavatories. The words 'Memorial Hall' over the door and a brass plaque gave details of the sad loss recalled now by few people. Land and possessions sold, the laird lived abroad for the rest of his days but left money for repairs and upkeep so the place remained pretty much the same as on its opening day in 1920. Meetings of the committee decided what colour new paintwork should be (light green, beige or pale blue perhaps); no one thought of replacing the print of a monster stag glaring over a mountain glen or the milder ones of sheep: people preferred to keep things as they were, in sepia.

The group of musicians for the Rose Queen Dance were in no way affected by restraint. John Grey regarded them glumly. The outfits were bad enough, garish T-shirts and very tight jeans, but why should hair be frizzed, dull and tangled as if it never saw comb or brush, or horror of horrors dyed pink! The drummer wore a large hat over his straggling locks; keyboard and guitar sported earrings and make-up. All were sallow-faced but moved with great energy. Misplaced? Would a war have straightened them out? Terrible thought! He steered Charlotte as far as possible from the deafening row; like him she must be wishing they were at home in the peace and quiet. Damn all social occasions.

She was in fact feeling guilty at letting John in for it, not being astute enough to sidestep the invitation, the honour much sought-after she was told of being asked to select a Rose Queen. Unlike some of the locals, the Greys, being newcomers, would be unbiased and give the choice more credibility, a fair choice of the fair! Maybe! And maybe she and John, green as grass, had been handed the hot potato!

Her upbringing was to blame for making the slightest social fib awkward. This warranted a full-blown bare-faced lie and she had been unable to rise or descend to it. A resolve to become a good liar was interrupted by someone asking her to dance: decibels prevented hearing what he was saying so she just smiled and nodded. It was an opportunity to see if a natural Queen of Roses gyrated anywhere near; no one at all, but she kept on looking.

After a few more ear-splitting numbers the group retired and a man of about 30 years of age, clasping a large accordion, stepped up on the stage to much applause, which he acknowledged with grace. Some cheers were for the music to come but perhaps his altogether splendid appearance came into it also: a jacket of midnight-blue velvet, snowy shirt with frothing lace at neck and sleeves, a very fine kilt, long cream socks, with a skean-dhu tucked in one, buckles of silver fronting his shoes. His naturally blond hair was short except where it fell in a sculptured wave low on the forehead. He was not sallow; a rather complacent smile gleamed in a fresh complexion. He did not wear earrings.

Most people got up to dance to a medley of Scottish tunes and the party took shape. Charlotte, forgetting the Rose Queen, began to enjoy herself. Her partner was large and portly and like most of that build light on his feet, an excellent dancer, skilful at finding space where young and old floated across the floor to the almost hypnotic rhythms. When the medley stopped there was an audible sigh of regret but not for long because the 'Gay Gordons' mustered. Charlotte went to look for John, thinking he might have felt left out of things and gone for a breath of air.

No! Dear John, not feeling out of things, was very much involved, a 'Gay Gordon' recruit in fact, with a female of that species laughingly instructing him as to the steps. Tall and willowy, her eyes almost on a level with his, she demanded attention, pouting, entwining him with slim white arms. Not that he was attempting escape, lolloping and swooping just like everybody else, or more so. Briefly it came into Charlotte's head to question whether the farming life sharpened basic instincts; she would not have minded swiping the fatuous look from his face. Keeping her smile intact she went to the ladies' cloakroom.

It was possible, but only just, to get through the door. The place was hardly big enough for a cluster of young women, one changing a skimpy black dress for a lavishly frilled and spotted red Spanish-style costume. In a lighthearted sort of way this girl was being teased about the exhibition dances she was getting ready for, but underneath the teasing was something else, a touch of resentment, even spite. Charlotte knew the girl to be a contender. She vaguely remembered hearing something, what was it? The school secretary with an eye for the schoolmasters, said to take them one by one as they arrived. Gossip! Shame if true but surely better than taking them on as a group? Anyway the other girls seemed to think her dancing would influence the judges. She made a mental note not to be influenced by flighty school secretaries in frilly dresses, particularly this one whose name was Melanie – Mel for short.

It was hard to get a look in at the mirror: they were sweet really, this gaggle of fussing girls, all just starting out, attractive or plain, average, medium, whatever they were. The door opened again with difficulty, but this time the entrant was not overlooked – it was Jeannie.

Coming in on a wave of perfume was the odds-on favourite, crowned four times already. Jeannie, married now with a baby

65

and all the more curvaceous for that. Jeannie was really lovely, tall, with good posture, abundant red-gold hair loosely curled. It looked like a case of 'Once more...' Another point in Jeannie's favour was good manners. She noticed Charlotte.

'Why, Mrs Grey isn't it? How are you?' She chatted easily and the others exchanged glances without much animus. 'Good old Jeannie, buttering up the judge!' All knew a winner when they saw one, also they wondered how long the woman had been there, and what had she heard?

'My uncle often speaks about you Mrs Grey, you know Ron Fox, your neighbour, my Uncle Ron? He says you've fairly done your place up well, very different to what it was with the new shed and all.'

Charlotte felt dismay. Ron Fox! Obstructive he'd been, unfriendly to the point of being hostile. A 'skate' in John's eyes. Crowning the man himself with something heavy would be more likely than John placing the rosebud wreath on this girl's beautiful head! She obviously had no idea about the skate/uncle's mean behaviour. So that was that! Some things are fated. Why hadn't they stayed at home, invented a crisis? She could have pretended to be ill, anything to avoid the coming moment, the choice...

She combed her own neat head and watched Jeannie ease red-gold strands to frame her face more perfectly, if that were possible, and by a mere fraction adjust her dress to allow the exuberant curves more freedom. Smiles from the others did not need analysing but Jeannie had not quite finished.

'That's a lovely dress Mrs Grey! You never got that from round here I guess!' The accent had an American overtone and little trace of the Doric. Was it seepage from the oilrigs or too many old films on the TV? A last look to check makeup particularly on a nose too dominant but giving character and an air of confidence. An old-time sailing ship might have had this girl as a figurehead proudly breasting the waves – literally too! Charlotte hastily put fancy aside and faced reality; she had to brief John.

As if on cue, John's 'Gay Gordon' came in: Fiona, second favourite, two to one against, worked in a dress shop. Blonde hair in a Sassoon type bob tossed in the accepted fashion. On catching sight of Jeannie, an instant of challenge zipped between the two, but Jeannie was quicker on the draw.

'I was just saying to Mrs Grey about her dress, not much chance around here for anything classic is there?'

Fiona made polite noises through slightly clenched teeth as Jeannie made an exit, score one–nil, the judge is my friend and your shop's not up to snuff. Not bad Jeannie, but your Uncle Ron doesn't help, and my dress is five years old.

John greeted her like a long-lost friend. 'Where on earth did you get to? I've looked everywhere!'

The accordion player was coming to the end of his stint, smiling but red in the face now rather than freshly pink. At the final chord of a lilting tune he gave a saucy little kick to sway the kilt and applause broke out as it always would. When he made way for the young men climbing on stage Charlotte drew John out of group-shot and gave him the news which had exactly the reaction foreseen.

'His niece? Foxy's?' Then meanly, 'Did you tell her that's the kiss of death in my book?'

'You can't talk like that John. It's not her fault.'

'Being related to a rat? A bloody great rat?' supplied John.

'She is a lovely girl John, quite the best-looking.'

'Well, she's had her turn and there are plenty more.'

'For instance, the one with the octopussy arms, your friend Fiona? She canvassed well!'

He looked bewildered then hastily innocent. 'I don't think ... I never noticed any such thing. Nice and friendly I thought!'

'She was! Just that! Having all those arms helps I should imagine!' The touch of venom was unexpected. He twisted at his collar, suddenly tight.

'Keep an open mind is all I ask. Wait for Mel and Jeannie. You ain't seen nuthin' yet!'

A breather seemed necessary and outside they found how some of the dancers had been fortified, men flushed and happy in reels that were more than robust, girls swung off their feet and laughing a lot. Lookers-on seemed very jolly too, crowding the main door, waggish, sometimes going too far: the laird long ago would not have approved. He had not allowed strong drink inside the Memorial Hall, but in the bicycle shed, in parked cars and spoiling the line of many a jacket was the liquid source of all the energy, the *bonhomie* and the less than nifty footwork. To his surprise John was hailed by Joe Waddell's son, usually silent and unforthcoming.

'Here Jimmy, ye'll tak' a dram wi' me!' Not wanting to quibble about a name John did, they knew one another all right. 'An the missus?' With a courtly gesture the bottle went to Charlotte who pretended to sip hoping he was too far gone to notice. It registered that ladies were not first in this set-up. More whisky from anchorman Tom, tug-of-war team, and from total strangers vodka, sherry, gin, martini, wine and eggnogg offered in great good humour, hospitality as generous as glasses to drink out of were scarce. Charlotte bowed to the necessity of taking a swig straight from a bottle, grasping the neck firmly so as not to offend. Was this the answer? Bigger sips from more bottles to save her from making one friend and a lot of enemies at midnight when the deed had to be done. The Rose Queen was to reign in the Howe for one whole year: no shared laurels, one beauty alone, one star, chosen by the two of them. She drank deep from the next bottle.

When they went back inside the accordion player took over again striking up a dreamy waltz to which they danced without being in accord, John happier after fresh air and a quenched thirst, Charlotte after magic in smaller doses merely putting on a smiling face. Then there were new people, several young men and partners coming in late, soon part of the swaying rhythm of the dance. Charlotte came alive in an urgent whisper to John. 'Look at the girl in the white dress!'

Rather sedate, dancing a little apart from the boy yet seeming unaware of anyone else, the girl was a white rose. She had large eyes with clear brows in a pale perfect complexion, hair that shone hanging straight and dark over the white dress. They moved to get closer and made an excuse to ask where the young couple came from. The boy answered, the girl smiling and quite shy. There was a luminous quality about her which was entrancing.

'Ballater. Thank God it's in the area.' John was delighted though he had taken the job much less seriously than Charlotte; didn't care too much about what people thought. 'So you can relax now madam, that little peach will do very nicely.' He swung Charlotte round with some enthusiasm then trod heavily on her toes: his dancing lesson hadn't helped much, she reflected, wanting very much to take off her shoe.

They enjoyed Melanie's display of really sultry Latin-American stuff. John enjoyed the excuse-me dances when he was much in demand. Mel, still in costume and mood, chose first but he could not quite follow the sudden changes of direction she led him into and the way she fixed him eye to eye was a bit much, made him blink. Went with the hobby he supposed or with the job at the school, kids nowadays hard to control. Next red-gold Jeannie, the only fault with this luscious armful her connection with the one man he couldn't stand. Perhaps, as Charlotte said, one should make allowances, it wasn't her fault, poor girl. He was rather careful with Fiona in case his wife's sardonic eye was on them but she did seem a good sort, anxious to improve the way he danced, probably had already...

At midnight Suzanne Mary in the white dress accepted with surprise a sash of rose-coloured silk: the rosebud wreath looked very pretty on her dark head. She was given a gift token for £20 and an additional voucher for £100 for clothes from the shop where Fiona worked. Charlotte hoped an assistant other than Fiona would help when that was spent. Mel had flounced out to change from the red costume as soon as the choice was announced. The finest response was Jeannie's. Her dazzling smile slipped then recovered, head held high she breasted the waves of dancers round Suzanne Mary, kissed her warmly on one cheek, the other and the first again as the luvvies do. Theatre it was without doubt and was applauded as such. There was a great buzz of talk during the last waltz.

Charlotte drove home because of John's tact in accepting so many drams.

'You have to be ver' careful not to offend the Scots,' he murmured contentedly.

When the road gave way to the narrower farm track their cows lifted pale faces at the familiar sound of the Land Rover, staring long after it passed before subsiding carefully next to sleeping calves. John was moved to speak again. 'It could've been a mistake you know Charlotte, choosing the li'l Ballater girl.' Charlotte pulled up on the close and got out, walking round to open his door as there seemed to be some difficulty with it.

'Go on then, tell me!'

The fresh air made an attack on him, the path not where it usually was. He rallied though. 'It was Jeannie an' Fiona an' the other one, they might've been very useful to me, to us I mean, sort of helpful, bein' local ... all of them seemed very ... helpful.' He wanted to make her see but couldn't quite remember what ... being so tired... He made a last attempt, taking great care to get the words right: 'You have to be so careful, ver' ver' carefu' so's not to offend...'

'...the locals. You said. Like Fiona and Jeannie and Mel. Pity they were so backward, didn't try really.' Her smile was enigmatic though he was unaware of it as she unlocked the door and walked through to the kitchen where sleepy cats yawned from the best chairs. She affected a painful limp. 'I'll just clean my teeth and the bathroom's yours!' Then in the nearest she could manage to the Doric: 'Tak' care whaur ye pit yir feet, Mr Astaire!' she said and climbed the stairs.

8

'He's whiles a richt ill-tricket kin 'o' wratch...'

The most important item on their shopping list was a bull and it needed a great deal of thought.

'Owners should realise that the bull is "half the herd" and take care that in selection and management this "half" is in no way neglected. Bulls should never be kept shut up in dark quarters... A bull should be given firm treatment always without either petting or teasing.'

This from the green book which John was reading aloud to Charlotte. 'Teasing? Did you say teasing?' Her bruised hands went to her face. 'I'll never get close enough!' She was more than apprehensive about the "half" still to come. She guessed John had a few qualms also but kept them to himself.

As ever he read all he could get his hands on, sought advice from the college, talked to people like Gilbert and his father, and listened.

Going to the bull sales in Perth had been the plan, but in February they were marooned. It was the same for Gilbert and his father who intended to go with him. They had all looked forward to seeing what breeders managed to put on show. The fashionable imports from Europe threatened all native breeds, particularly the old 'Aberdeen Angus'; there was a good deal of talk about that. John wanted to see the breeds, find out what was adjudged best in each class and of course get an idea of the price.

From the book again: 'In order to achieve a calving index of 365 days it is necessary to get the cows in calf between the eighth and twelfth week after calving.' Anna and Gertie and other cows were nearing this sort of deadline, so 'St George,' the name suggested for the champion and progenitor of a Burnside herd, must be chosen and brought home soon.

Gilbert, familiar with the idea of a tight calving index, still had doubts. 'I'm not saying it's wrong John but I'm nae sure it applies to the situation we hiv here. First an' foremost it wid seem daft tae be up on the hill calvin' in the storms again, as ye were. Ye cannot wish that, folks. Say the bull goes in aboot the first week in June in some places, some time in July would be OK up here, or, a wee bittie later even. Mak' yir ain rule tae suit yirsel.' The voice of reason as always from Gilbert and it meant they would have more time to decide.

Journeys away from the farm were rare in this new life, but on a day when no calf was due and a very early inspection confirmed a calving was unlikely, they drove to Aberdeen to keep an appointment. They were to see Alastair, an adviser at the college who took an interest in their venture from the start, visiting bearing gifts when the farm was cut off from 'civilisation'. In the farm diary they had a very good picture of him and a friend taken that day, bearing a rather understated 'came to tea' caption. Seeing him again would be pleasant.

Referring to John's Alfa-Romeo exchanged for a Land Rover a friend had written: 'We miss that Red Streak'. The Land Rover, higher than most cars and giving a noisier ride, unlikely to be stolen from a car park for any quick getaway did not streak but had other uses. However this morning John had to brake suddenly and come to a stop because round a corner ambling in the middle of the road came a large, very large it seemed to Charlotte, black bull.

'Come on, Charlotte, we'll have to do something! It might get killed or cause an accident!' He jumped out and looked in the hedgerow for some kind of stick to wave or extend his reach, but there was not so much as a twiglet. With reluctance Charlotte got down. No other traffic on the road, never the case when he drove the Red Streak. The large black animal looked up, halting slightly ahead of them. Seen closer even Charlotte could not detect any hostility.

'Well now laddie, hadn't you better go back the way you came?' John was using his steading voice, soft and persuasive, practised on Gertie and her like. Charlotte could not help a fleeting wish he could sound less English; the bull might listen more to the Doric. In any case it made no difference to 'laddie' who stood stock still and flickered brandy-ball eyes at them. They returned the scrutiny.

John ended it by loudly stamping his feet and going forward with arms out wide. Charlotte, within an ace of leaping back into the Rover, managed not to but screened by the door was rather less than brave. As if he never could fathom the ways of men, with a strangled sort of snort the bull turned clumsily to do as John suggested in the first place. They followed slowly; still no traffic. Well ahead on the right-hand side of the road John spotted an opening, a wooden gate slewed across it.

'There's his home!' He increased speed to catch up then slowed to pass, giving as wide a berth as possible, coming to a stop just beyond the gate. Seeing two people blocking the way ahead the bull veered and pushed his way back into the field. 'Just right laddie!' John was pleased. They rescued the damaged gate and made a fair attempt to secure it. 'Go and tell them at the farmhouse. About a hundred yards round the corner I think. This will never hold, needs more.' He grinned, 'Unless you would rather look after him while I go?' Charlotte was off, already yards down the road. She vaguely remembered a house where John said, with a nice garden and some trees. She really missed lush trees now; their English garden had a lot.

There was a wide front door but she went to the back as was customary and knocked. A pleasant-looking woman came. Charlotte took a breath after hurrying. 'Er, something of an emergency I'm afraid. We were coming along and a bull was on the road, a long way back. We put him in a field but the gate's broken.' She stopped. 'Will it be your bull? We didn't know.'

'Aye! he'll be oor bull. He'll likely dae that! Brak oot! Jis' so!' She seemed unworried. Smiling she asked, 'An fit like at Burnside? I ken ye fairly git the snaw mair than doon here, bit it's a bonny place i' the summer time.' A tall man crossed the yard and she broke off to call, 'It's yon bull! The aul' de'il's awa' up the road! Ye'll hiv tae sort that gate noo!' The reaction was so calm and matter of fact it made Charlotte ashamed of cowering behind the Rover. No one except John had seen and she was bound to hear more about it from him, yet surely it was a bit out of the ordinary, a bull just taking a stroll?

They talked more, asked Charlotte to take 'a fly cup' but she explained about the appointment in the city. John had parked on the verge across the gateway as a double safeguard though the bull was grazing quietly in mid-field. The farmer thanked John and excused the bull.

'He's a quiet boy, the aul' Angus. Gittin' on a bit in years an' nae problem, nae really!'

With a touch of mischief he addressed Charlotte, smiling, having summed things up pretty accurately. 'Ye ken, ye could ride on 'is back missus!'

He saluted cheerily as they drove off. Charlotte, brushing mud from her skirt, murmured to John, 'Don't put money on it!'

On their way were fields with grazing animals almost to the boundary; then the city crematorium, a modern housing estate, a school, a tree-lined entrance to a public park and on a wider road houses of some consequence, the approach to the true granite city.

It was a pity most of these good stone buildings sparkling in the sunlight now were offices – oil, insurance, finance, law. When they were built how different life must have been for the prospering citizens, their large families, the servants who looked after them all. If they could see, if ever in the dusk they returned as shades, searching for what was no more, wandering through the silent offices, fingering electronic machines.

Charlotte came back to the present as they left Queen Victoria at the roundabout. She looked at her watch.

'There's no time for Union Street, but it doesn't matter.' John was relieved because he still 'looked at baith sides o' a bawbee' as the saying went. He disliked the drag of that street, which in his opinion suffered from a general blight of garish modern shopfronts and chain-stores, the same wherever you went. You had only to look up to see it had been fine-looking before they brought it up to date.

They picked up bags of sugar beet nuts and mineral blocks from a farmers' co-operative, and then drove down the esplanade to the sea and a parking spot at Footdee, the old fishermen's quarter. It was pleasant there, just the place for sandwiches and a flask of tea and watching boats move to and from the harbour. Charlotte had read that in the last century Footdee women ruled the community ('the men had nothing to do but catch the fish' and 'The women enslave the men to their will and keep them enchained under petticoat government'). As far as she knew farmers' wives inland had never cottoned on.

John drove back along the seafront, carefully observing a speed limit ignored by some. Charlotte remarked, 'There never seems to be anyone bathing, dogs splash in and out but not the owners and it's such a marvellous stretch of sand.'

'Nothing to stop you, next time,' John offered. 'Except it could be a bit cold?'

With Alastair they quickly got down to business – bull business. He took the point of putting the bull in later at Burnside. It made sense unless they were aiming at the autumn sales when an older animal would have more weight.

'No! We're keeping them on after weaning, over-wintering and selling when people want something to put on their summer grass. Demand should be firm then if we can hold out. I'm taking more hay and I have room in the courts. Also it would clear the turnips earlier, better than this time when so many were rotten before I could get at 'em. Due to the foul weather of course. If neeps were not such a good feed I would question whether it paid me to grow them. But back to the bull...'

Alastair was thoughtful. 'It has to be direct from the breeder now, but who?' Tactfully he went on, 'Important to have a guid-tempered beast, easy to handle, no point in making life harder than ye need.' Then slyly, 'Also there's Charlotte to consider, if she takes up riding ... but seriously, there's a point.' He thought for a spell: 'Ye spoke of having room in the court, and it gave me an idea I'll put before ye.' He took a sip of coffee. 'Ye know Willie Maclean at Carnegie where ye bought cows already in calf by his bulls, right? Well, Willie has bulling heifers to sell just now. A chap in the office told me they were toppers, like all Carnegie stock o' course.' They were paying close attention. 'It's worth a thought. If you bought his bulling heifers, or some of them even, I reckon ye'd get the offer of a bull from Willie, to rent maybe at so much a head, or in exchange for keepin' the beast housed and fed for the winter. Ye could make the arrangement, whichever suited!' He warmed to the theme. 'I suggest it shelves the bull problem, saves his purchase money or better still uses it to bring in cash. There's the option of selling a few months later as 'in-calf heifers' or if not, ye've increased the herd an' get the subsidies in due course.'

John considered. 'I've dismissed the idea of renting because of introducing any risk – yet with Willie's bulls this doesn't arise, we have their progeny and are well pleased, all strong and healthy so far.'

Charlotte was looking at her watch. 'We'll have to make a move John, it's later than we planned.'

He stood. 'We'll have to mull it over

Alastair, but the cows are waiting! I really appreciate your help. Will discuss with the boss of course.'

Charlotte smiled. 'I reckon you've put the cat amongst the pigeons Alastair. Thanks for the coffee and everything. We'll be in touch!' She picked up her handbag and glanced at them both. 'I am *not* the boss, but I know about the women of Footdee, so watch out!'

'Rentabull' occupied them totally as they drove in heavier evening traffic past the fine houses where the shades were just beginning to assemble.

9

'A bull's best faced an' lookit i' the ee...'

It was settled. They were to have not one of the Carnegie bulls but two! The decision was practical but in the wee small hours when Charlotte lay awake panic took over. Faint-hearted, lily-livered, yellow she applied scathingly to herself, but all were true: she wanted most of all to escape back to the old life. During the day she affected nonchalance, but no one was deceived. John said she need have very little to do with the bulls, he would cope and Gilbert promised help when it was necessary. So now they were on their way to choose heifers.

The first time they visited Mains of Carnegie the grieve had been sent to meet them. He waited in a lay-by outside the nearest village and they followed him it seemed for miles and miles along twisting narrow roads past acres of farmland where the spring growth was already lush. A spasm of jealousy struck John to see how the fertile well-farmed land contrasted with Burnside.

Without a guide it was more difficult, and somewhere in the maze they took a wrong turning. John hating to be late grew edgy as he always did, using sailor's language when tractors chug-chugging too close together blocked his way. A towed caravan well away from the verge was the last straw. 'John! You lack patience! This isn't the M1!'

'It would be all the same with a moron like that, he'd still be driving in the middle of the bloody road!' He was flushed and angry by the time they drew up in front of the Mains' imposing house.

Maclean was a prosperous man: he had inherited farms and added more and more land round them, so he had considerable acreage. He had the reputation of breeding the best suckler cows in the North, animals of outstanding quality with high price tags. For anyone setting up a herd these cows were an investment they would be unlikely to regret. John, who could not afford to make mistakes, felt well satisfied at buying from Willie Maclean.

It must be said that the man had been intrigued when they met, the two of them with no farming background or experience giving up as he saw it friends, family, a life of ease in the soft English climate for (he was too polite to say) a hill-billy farm at the back of beyond. Large, dressed in comfortable rather loud tweeds, Maclean was quietly spoken, with a ponderous manner. 'I can't help wondering, forgive my curiosity, what motivated you to do something so...?'

'Crazy?' smiled John. A lot of people were curious, some believed they had fled from a 'rat race'; then there was the 'Londoner with money to burn' school of thought, a sourish taste that left, but on reflection the rumours could have had a more sinister tinge. So far as they knew nobody suspected them of anything shady – one look at John spelled Royal Navy and traditional values; Charlotte was sometimes thought 'uppity'. An answer had evolved which most people accepted readily given the genuine attachment of the Scots to their country.

'Coming to Scotland was returning to our roots, both Charlotte and I have Scottish blood, her mother and my grandfather; it seemed a natural thing to do.' This was true but had little to do with the move. It did not satisfy a man like Maclean.

'But surely you could have done something else in your own line, in Edinburgh perhaps. Why farming? A hard life. I think very different from what you've been used to, especially you Mrs Grey?' John, making a judgement of the man, told the truth, confessed a long-held ambition common to a good many people in the service.

'There's this yarn, you know, where you carry an anchor, as far inland as you can and when people say "What's that?" you settle!'

Charlotte answered the unspoken question as Willie turned to her. 'Not me! I had no wish to farm. Basically I just came along! I'm keen now except for bulls, John will tell you!'

He was silent for a moment or two, looking very serious. Then, 'I admire ye both,' he said simply.

John smiled.

'I must be a gambler, with about as little sense.' With a straight look he added, 'But it had to be tried rather than spend my days regretting, and my wife was kind.'

'May the gamble succeed! I wish you well, both of you!' he said warmly and shook hands on it. He took great pains showing the breeding cows, pointing out what he judged to be suitable for them and saying why. He consulted Sandy, the grieve, giving careful attention to his opinions, and making it plain that he wanted John and Charlotte to be given the best attention. That was how they came by their fine cows and gained a friend.

They gained two friends in fact. No one else was quite like Sandy. 'This lad is my right-hand and most of the left one as well,' Willie declared. Smallish, with a nut-brown face and clear eyes brimming with enthusiasm, Sandy was a mine of information, nothing was too much trouble to do or explain. He worked impossible hours, seeming to need little sleep, his attention to detail extraordinary. Willie was lucky in this man and knew it.

The Macleans were away in America on holiday so the heifers were shown off by Sandy. 'Ye'd niver regret buyin' this lot John, the same breedin' exactly as yir ain coos. Toppers, they are, the hale lot o' them! Jis' look, the same mithers and the same sire, as like as peas in a pod!' More peas! But they were beautiful, younger versions of the cows at Burnside and would match up perfectly. How did you choose, though, from the 14 and what about those left over? They formed a natural group like a miniature herd already; it would be a pity to split them up. John was visualising his bank statement, wondering if he dare afford them all. The decision came from Charlotte.

'We'll have them Sandy, all fourteen.'

A few days later a telephone call from Sandy told them he was coming down to see his mother who lived in a village a few miles from their farm. He would like to bring them the young bull, the one for the heifers. He would use a horsebox on his vehicle. The heifers would have to wait until a float came back from England in a day or so. Meanwhile they could have the bull and it would be a good idea to keep him inside for a wee while, give him a chance to get used to them both. And vice-versa thought Charlotte. So if it was OK? This evening? John prepared a place in the court.

As they waited Charlotte wrote an overdue letter, breaking off when the Range Rover appeared towing a horsebox slowly up the farm road. John went out alone and then came back with Sandy. The bull was installed in his temporary home and given hay and a few sugar beet nuts for a welcome. All without fuss. Sandy did not want to eat as his mother liked to cook supper for him, but he sat with them and had a cup of tea. When he got up to go John went out to the close to help as he reversed and turned, tricky enough as a manoeuvre.

It gave time for a postscript to the letter:

All accomplished, though not by me.
John says he is a big bull but he walked inside like a lamb. That would be Sandy's training – he is marvellous with animals, very quiet always. The bull is called Charley, has a fancy pedigree but Sandy says all bulls should be called Charley. So much for St George and England. I may take a discreet look tomorrow – through binoculars – or a telescope??? Love, Ch.

She sealed and stamped the envelope and went to put it ready for the postman who collected as well as delivered mail. There was a noise, or had she imagined it? At the back window? Not very likely but she went to have a look, opening it to peer out. At the same time Charley thrust a massive curly head through, peering in! They would have bumped had she not leapt back like a startled hare! He gave a funny little snort which ended almost as a whimper when very rapidly indeed she left his field of vision. After Charley was replaced in his den, Sandy explained:

'The puir beast probably missed all his

companions at hame ye ken. Wis fairly bewildered in a strange place an' lonely. Thocht he wid ging tae look.'

'And found Charlotte, of all people!' John could not help laughing.

Sandy was anxious to reassure. 'He will-nae git oot agin, he is secure, I promise! There is nae cause tae worry, an' he really is a very quiet bull.'

Still trembling, Charlotte gulped down the drink John poured. In a quavery sort of trance she had stood blocking one line of escape with John opposite guarding the way down the farm road. Sandy, talking softly, had walked the bull away from the house. At one moment Charlotte fancied a lumbering step in her direction, she saw brandy-ball eyes blinking in the light from the doorway, but Sandy had kept him straight. And now all was safe, they said. She held out the glass for more brandy. 'Just tell Alcoholics Anon I'll be in touch!' she said. 'Before Charley Two comes!'

10

'Am I no' a bonny fighter...?'

Unfortunately on the way back from England the Maclean float was involved in an accident on the Al. Nothing serious, nobody hurt but repairs were going to take about a week. So Sandy had telephoned to ask: could John wait for the heifers or should a local haulier bring them at a cost of £30 or £40 at the most? The thought of spending money was apt to give John indigestion and it suited him to wait for the same reason as before; he did not want early calving, especially of heifers. But, there was Charley, still inside and growing fat...

John and Gilbert leaned on the gate and watched the bull move his bulk from the hay-haik and sink heavily to the deep straw of his bed, expelling a great gust of air like steam from a locomotive. His jaws began a contented roll, his eyes, seeming half-closed, were in fact responsive to the slightest movement; his coat had a healthy shine. There were no behaviour problems; he had not ventured out to play peek-a-boo with Charlotte. Now and again she walked over to look at him but never on her own. She had to concede that since the fateful evening of his debut he had been, well, quiet.

In the far distance Lochnagar gleamed with its necessary snow; on the hill gorse blazed a fierce gold. Only little sounds disturbed the somnolence of the afternoon: truly the 'bonny days' had come. Calving was finished except for a pure Aberdeen Angus cow not yet due. The old ewes with lambs; the neep field ready for sowing; sufficient grass everywhere and no need for feeding, except for Charley. Ah Charley! A mistake you made accepting the lift with Sandy! Yet the bull was only a speck in an ocean of content as they recovered from the travail of winter, though looking at the great black bulk of him it would be tempting to say 'Some speck!'

Gilbert gave an opinion as he studied the bull. 'I believe he needs tae be oot o' there and grazin' John. Feedin' himself. Not waited on like a Prince at Balmoral.'

John knew this to be true. 'It's just a question of where, Gilbert. Where do I put him? The park where he's going with his heifers is too far away, I could never keep my eye on him away down there. It is the best-fenced, all newly done, but too far away for him on his own. I'm afraid to risk him up here where he might get through to the cows so I have to keep him inside, though I don't like it, not one bit.'

A grin from Gilbert. 'Among the many books ye hiv in that office o' yours I noticed one we hid in so-called "Liberal Studies": the hale o' this course wis meant tae broaden the mind an' ye'll ken fit it did for me... Bit ye micht use a wee bit o' lateral thinkin' on yir bull?'

'By God, you're right! De Bono! Now how do I tackle this one? I can't move Charley too far away but I can move the girls. I move not him but them? Some job shifting them all but in that park they'd be OK to wait for the second bull. Charley gets the heifers up here when they come and meantime can go on the hill.' He frowned as a thought came. 'The only snag would be if anything went wrong with a cow or calf, it would be difficult to bring...' His face cleared. 'No! Think positive. They move, not the boy-o.'

'We'll easy dae that! Tomorrow? I'll be doon early as I can manage.'

Later Charlotte raised a point. 'About

Charley John. Hasn't he got an awful lot of space on the hill? To be loose in?' She could picture the bull rampaging wild and free, herself a trembling hostage marooned in the kitchen. John would like the Aga used 24 hours a day to produce what he called 'big eats'.

Unaware of this reflection John explained. 'Gilbert thinks he will stay fairly close to the source of his food, even with grass to nibble he'll be interested in the beet nuts; we'll continue giving him those so he'll come back at night and to his bed. It's a bit like the Spanish *querencia* – a special sort of place for him.' Her face registered doubt so he gave up and went to put things ready for the morning.

The next morning Gilbert tried. 'If he still gits a puckle o' hay an' the sugar beet he'll likely come back. Whyivver not? I prom...'

'Don't Gilbert! No promises, don't tempt fate! All I know is that I'll be the one who's cooped up!' She warmed to the idea of martyrdom, seeing she was having some effect on Gil. John of course knew her too well. Her voice was forlorn. 'I'll never dare go on the hill now, not with Charley on the loose!' There was truth behind the pathos.

Gilbert felt compelled to bring the matter

up again. 'There is a snag if he went up that brae there John, at the top where the march fence is weak. That neebor o' yours is a lazy b–. The state o' his fences! Maybe he'll grudge the money when he's nae beasts up there. Ye must hope an' pray he dis'nae get heifers from onywhere seeing the bull's not busy! It's been done afore I'll tell ye, mentioning no names!'

Having a reshuffle, moving a herd of cows from one place to another. Simple? It could be. Call the boss cow or leader to bring the others to the gate, stay with them there until every beast has cottoned onto the idea that a move is afoot, no stragglers, all assembled. Then move off to the new location, to 'pastures new', literally. One person could do it, although two would be nice.

Having a reshuffle, moving a herd with calves at foot. Simple? Never, never, never! Burnside had seen a few moves end stormily in words better left unsaid. After the last one Charlotte absolutely refused to speak to John, the silence like a pall over them magnifying and prolonging the loss of harmony. She brooded. If she really were a congenital idiot it was interesting she was the one prepared to support his crazy idea. She did know her left hand from her right, an honest mistake it had been, not a crime! And there was no need to swear! On John's part he wondered how he could possibly be an unfeeling selfish brute when he spent his whole life looking after the bloody cows, like a bee in a bottle buzzing round after them. And a light smack across the rear end did not make a case for the SSPCA. Charlotte could be very unreasonable. He lifted heavy gates back from where they had been fixed to limit access to the wrong places. Normally she would have helped but had flounced into the house.

Conscious of letter-writing as a sort of catharsis Charlotte decided to devote time to answering those from friends in the south. At the same time she would hurt John's enormous appetite by not preparing food. Serve him right! He could have bread and cheese! She had to guard against revealing her present state of mind though, it would not take much for rumour to spread like wildfire round the old gang. Of course, Victor might drive to the rescue in his white Bentley! It restored her a little to think of that.

She wrote about moving cows:

It really is some operation, much more complicated when there are small calves. You see cows all have this fantastic mothering in-stinct (better than some we both know) and the calves now are likely to gang up together, inclined to ignore mothers calling them to heel. So, when we have a move the first priority is to get them all, the whole lot, at the gate. It involves someone, usually me, acting as sheepdog to round up stragglers (better than keep-fit class) and then John opens the gate. All well so far. John leads with the boss cow and they all stream off, the stragglers and me bringing up the rear. Easy, you must think? Well it isn't unless you have a road with walls about ten feet high to confine them and we certainly haven't. This is where it usually starts to go horribly wrong.

1 The calves are thrilled to be free; one starts a joyous gallop and careers along, heels kicking, tail held at a ridiculous angle, head – well round here there is an expression 'high heided' for anything or anyone (!) on the frisky side. Of course the maverick is followed by others of the same age with the same tremendous muscle power and they're off! They outstrip the drover.

2 Meanwhile at the rear one or two mothers have just had a change of mind; torn between the desire to play follow-my-leader and a suspicion that their particular darling has

been left behind, mother-love wins and they decide to go back to check, easily dodging the panting drover's mate. Get the picture?

What does the DM do? Go back and chase the neurotics or keep going? I can tell you neither works.

3 Do not forget the middle band, average worthy cows whose only wish is to do the right thing, follow the boss, do what the drover wants, etc. etc. These cows are a little bewildered at the way things are developing, possibly they may have very young calves sticking like limpets to them. Raising a little moan or two as the pace quickens they catch the excitement of bolder spirits whose bonnets are already over the windmill. Shall we? they wonder. Dare we? Would it be nice?

4 The boss cow and her cronies: Ho! Ho! they think. What rollicking fun this is! How the kids are enjoying themselves! Must join in! Harumph! Galumph! Away we go! (It may be awa' we ging!)

5 The drover: knackered would describe him.

6 His mate: the same. Scarlet in the face. Dishevelled, hair like Medusa's. Temper fragile. Will be reaching for the brandy.

7 Enquiries: will be ignored or get a dusty answer.

What a letter! Hope I haven't bored you to death. Not the intention. Much love from the Sheepdog/DM/bullwatcher etc., and from John. Am about to cook a massive meal for us both.

With Gilbert on the strength the current move had a brighter look to it. John had been at work blocking off every possible avenue of escape; gates were fixed across openings, tractor, cart, muckspreader, Land Rover all strategically positioned; a place allotted for Gil's vehicle. The route was out-lined with only the hill vulnerable to creative moves by anything on four legs.

It was accomplished. Not perfectly – there was some effective sprinting on the high ground as expected; a few spates of naval language evoking a little moral tut-tutting; a fresh insight into the Doric as a means of expression; some heavy sarcasm and one devastating dagger-look between husband and wife; but it was a definite improvement. Relaxation over a good meal and then all that remained was to offer Charley his freedom.

He did not want it. Stayed on the straw bed, cudding, eyeing the outside world for a long time before deciding to sample what it seemed to promise. When he heaved his black bulk onto neat small feet, he took only a few steps to graze the nearest patch of grass. As Gilbert predicted he returned to 'hame', and the beet nuts left there, long before dusk dimmed the bright gorse and softened the brash outline of the new steading.

The quiet bull was still on his bed when John took the 'puckle' hay ration before going off to inspect the cows and calves in their new pasture. Charlotte looked through binoculars later, seeing him grazing as before, near 'hame'. By lunchtime she reported he was 'exploring' a bit so John followed and found him 'just grazing'. This became the pattern of Charley's days and he always returned to the comfort of deep straw in his *querencia* before dusk. A routine evolved of strolling round the herd in the early evening and checking Charley last. Alongside the new pasture a path led over the hill towards his shelter and here John would leave Charlotte to return to the house alone. Until one evening when the scents of gorse and broom and short cropped grass and dried earth drifted towards her, and it seemed absurd not to take the path and enjoy the hill again. She called out 'Wait for me John, I'm coming.'

They climbed easily, knowing every inch of the way, around them the air fresh and sweet and the sound of water burbling in the little streams that made the hill such a good place for cattle. A handsome cock pheasant eyed them and his hens scuttered out of their way; they disturbed the usual rabbits. Then they had the shock of their lives.

Towards the boundary fence, which sagged noticeably providing an easy step-over, was Charley! A snorting, stamping, threatening Charley, cursing it seemed a replica of himself, another black bull snorting and threatening and cursing back! There was no time to do anything. They were helpless as the two launched themselves. Cr-aack! Solid bone met solid bone, heads locked, the battle was on!

It was fearsome to see. The idea is to get the head underneath the enemy's head, jerk, topple him, force him down onto his side, vulnerable to blows, to continued blows, the weapon always the massive head. Straining, gasping, grunting they drew apart momentarily, maybe to get breath, and John was horrified to see Charlotte whip off her light jacket and, shouting like a demon, hurl herself at Charley, who, blessed relief, retreated a few steps. She flapped the jacket hard across his face, stinging his eyes so he had to turn away. John leapt to help. Yelling and flapping they forced the black bull down the rough path. Stumbling, groaning, he abandoned the fight, a victim of the cape, the *toreros* victorious. At a cautious distance they were followed.

They got to the steading and Charley was in, doors bolted. Thinking of the second warrior, Charlotte began 'Shall we?' She was interrupted by a snarling John, angrier than she had ever seen him.

'Don't,' he spat, 'don't *ever* do that again! Don't dare! You acted like a bloody fool!'

'But...'

'No effing buts. You of all people!' Rage consumed him, and exasperation. 'You don't seem to realise you could've...'

Her turn to interrupt. 'But I wasn't!' With emphasis and grinning hugely, 'I *wasn't* and it *worked!*' She was still on a high, getting her breath back, persistent. 'So what about the other?'

'Leave the bastard!' John stamped off into the house.

The second bull was sniffing at the steading doors by now, Charley no doubt breathing heavily at the other side. Charlotte watched, triumph evaporating, her knees taking on the familiar wobble. It was hard to believe she had been so...?

John came back. He had telephoned and been brusque. 'You'd better come for your bull. Now, from my farm. And I do mean now!' He had slammed down the phone, realising he hadn't spoken like that to anyone since leaving the service, excepting Charlotte perhaps when they moved the cows. Like the quiet bull, John Grey had another side.

A shamefaced man employed by Ron Fox and half a dozen of his cronies collected the bull and ambled behind him down the farm road. No reference was made to the broken fence; no explanation or apology offered.

John remained quiet as they sat in the kitchen with the comfort of a pot of tea. Charlotte had thought of whisky but decided not to risk offering. After a while he was amazed to see her shoulders move with suppressed laughter. He could think of nothing to laugh about. She turned to him, putting her cup shakily on its saucer.

'John, I've had a dreadful thought! The bulls, they were going round a bit, staggering round as they fought. Could I? Do you think I?'

'Come on, Charlotte, spit it out. What are you saying?' She looked at him, wanting him to share the terrible joke.

'Could I, I mean do you think it possible that I frightened the wrong one?'

It was a pleasure to see Sandy check over the bull making sure he was not damaged in the fight. Charley was secured between gates in the steading and did not object to Sandy's careful hands, probing, lifting his feet, examining and treating small cuts and bruises on his head. As a final touch and with a comic flourish, seeing that Charlotte was watching, he took scissors out of his bag and with little finger delicately poised snipped briskly to remove extra long hair from the inside of Charley's ears!

'That's you laddie, bonnie as ivver an' ready tae fecht again! A cut an' blaw dry for the lugs!' He blew into the tough black flaps. Charley did not mind, he was used to Sandy.

Charlotte exchanged a look with John, knowing what he was thinking. It had been unnecessary, the terrible doubt she raised. In effect she had collared the nearest bull in the fading light. Neither of them could be sure, and when they went to have a look it was too dark, the bull still unsettled. Though he looked like Charley it meant nothing, the warriors had been a matched pair, snorting mirror images before that murderous clash of skulls.

Back in the kitchen they had half expected a call from Fox, while knowing it unlikely the men had done anything except push the collected bull into some shed until morning. They had gone to bed but were unable to sleep, sometimes hysterical with invention: bulls could be swapped at dawn, they would creep into enemy territory to do it, hoping Fox was a heavy sleeper, the worse for wear after a night at the pub. Or despondent, thinking of Sandy annoyed and angry at them: 'Hoo could ye John mak' sic' a bluidy feel hash?' Explaining Charlotte as a dervish whirling into attack would never have the ring of truth.

John was more certain the real Charley was in the steading when they spent time looking at him in daylight. It was confirmed when they opened the doors and like a vessel making harbour he ambled over to the cart shed and sank with a huge sigh onto his bed.

11

Impasse

The fight was not Charley's fault. His trans-mutation from 'quiet' to 'demon fighter' was down to Ron Fox and the unrepaired fence, but getting together with the man to discuss this was not easy. They rarely met casually, as with Joe or any other neighbour. Telephone messages went unanswered so it was necessary to go and seek him out or, more aptly, run him to earth. Walking briskly John stepped over his own fence and then skirted a rough pasture keeping to where he supposed an old track had been. Soon he found himself at the back door of the Braehead farmhouse and was lifting a hand to the lion-head knocker when the door opened smartly and an old lady who had most likely watched his approach snapped out a disconcerting 'Yes?' The knife in her hand did not suggest welcome. John looked nothing like a travel-ling salesman, had a more outdoor aspect and did not wear violent aftershave; neither were his clothes smart enough, though narrowly better than a burglar's or tinker's. He hoped she could judge that and put the weapon down.

'Good afternoon,' he began, meeting the hostile stare which yet had a mite of something like curiosity in it. He persevered. 'My name is Grey, John Grey from Burnside down there,' he waved towards his house and regretted not being there drinking a cup of tea with Charlotte. 'I'm wondering whether...'

'He's oot!' The words slashed across before he finished. Then a curt demand rather than a question: 'Ye'll come in!' With polite thanks John followed her into a room which had no acquaintance with 'designers' or 'fitments' or 'units'. In this kitchen everything was simple and functional and on a generous scale. The high-banked fire in the oven range had boiled a kettle still hissing at the end of a polished steel sweigh; the dresser crammed with bright plates and dishes had the lovely patina of age-old household things; there were copper pans on an oval of cast iron suspended from the beamed ceiling; thick wooden shelves held named pots for rice, sugar, flour and tea but not coffee, John noticed. Everything was shining and clean. He smiled in appreciation, turning to the old lady. 'Forgive me for looking so closely, but this is such a rare kitchen, just the sort of place I like; my wife too, she would love it.' His voice tailed off because she was not listening. She in her turn was staring, sizing up the alien standing at her hearth.

She was quite formidable, not by any means the little old lady of sentiment but strong, broad-shouldered, her eyes on a level with his, and he was no midget. Her hair was tightly drawn back and no wayward tendrils escaped from it. As she fixed him with eyes still fine and dark her brows were in an uncompromising line, like that of her thin-lipped mouth. Abruptly she spoke.

'A wis aboot tae hiv ma fly-cup,' she announced, 'and ye're welcome tae jine me.' She thumped two mugs from the dresser onto the square white-scrubbed table and, as an afterthought, tumblers and a bottle of malt whisky out of a polished corner cupboard. From the teapot waiting in its cosy on a hob at the side of the range she poured tea which came out thick and black. 'Mulk?' she queried. 'Sugar?' John refused the sugar because he did not see any and by implication it might be an indulgence. Charlotte had the same attitude on occasions when he

111

added a few spoonfuls to give him energy. He watched as an amount of whisky splashed into the tumblers and she raised hers, murmuring an unintelligible toast. His 'Er, cheers!' sounded pretty feeble. By what was left in her glass he could tell she was no slouch at taking the 'water of life' and wondered if her son approved, and should he happen to walk in right now what would he think of John's sharing this 'fly-cup'.

As if reading his thoughts she leaned across the table. She had fumbled in the pocket of a flowered pinafore for tiny metal-rimmed spectacles which she clamped on a rather aggressive nose. 'He's nae my son, Ronald, ye ken. Mairriet my girl mair's the pity, bit she's deid these mony yeers puir quine.' A pause to confirm she had guessed right about his mistake. 'Tho' Ronald,' the name was a sneer, 'wid like fine tae fergit it, this is my hoose an' nae his, an' maistly its my ferm an' nae his, so mebbe its masel' ye need tae spik 'til and nae him, ower the fence?' Belatedly he recognised the malice in the fine eyes but could not tell whether it targeted him or Ronald. Certainly her son-in-law was not her pride and joy. It didn't make the situation any clearer.

'Nevertheless, Mrs...'

'Grace, Hannah Grace, born i' this hoose, mairriet ma cousin Will, also deid this mony a yeer.' The grandfather clock in the corner had a sonorous tick which had counted out the minutes, the hours and the days, with only Hannah left. She went on, her expression closed in, grim. 'Ower twa hunnert yeers sin' oor fowk hid the ingang. Brak maist o' the grun fae the heather an' fairmed in gweed times an' bad.' It fascinated John to hear her: what a tale she could tell if they were friends and not opposed as she confirmed. 'An we hid nae fancy muckle sheds.' He took it on the chin.

'Nevertheless, Mrs Grace, it's fencing I've come about as you seem to understand, so if your *son-in-law*,' he gave this emphasis 'sees to that I'd better discuss it with him!' He got to his feet and was thanking her for the hospitality when she stopped him, her voice rather softer, almost conciliatory.

'Och sett ye doon mannie, I reckon we hiv a'thing tae spik aboot yet!' Before he could stop her another monster dose splashed into his glass and he had to do as she said. He wondered if Ron ever summoned the courage to disobey. She was staring again across the table and it made him feel nervous. 'Ronald says yir lady keeps hersel' tae hersel'; bonny eneuch bit snooty. Feerly posh is she? Yon's the spik.' The bright malicious eyes waited, her back was ramrod straight in the kitchen chair. He had to laugh.

'No, Mrs Grace, you could not be more wrong. My wife is the best in the world: just as you were for your man I expect. Mind you, I can't answer for her opinion of your son-in-law, maybe she, well, doesn't like him for some reason?'

A little twitch at the corner of the thin mouth, further scrutiny and then, 'Ma ither dochter's dochter kens the baith o' ye, wis feerly ta'en wi' you mister, thocht ye a fine braw mannie bit wis neen ower pleased aboot ye chusin' that ither wee-bit lassie at the dance. Wis it yir wife's deein' then?' Startlingly clear came the image of the beauty who mentioned being the niece of Ron Fox, those splendid curves and the height, that beak of a nose – a legacy! He laughed again: anyone daring to overlook grandmama as Rose Queen of her day would have been clobbered there and then. He tried to dismiss the certainty and made an overture.

'I must say Mrs Grace I can see a strong resemblance between you and your grand-daughter.' It was the truth though she ignored the compliment and mocked him.

'An I must say mister ye hiv a fine seam o' teeth, aa yir am a' wid reckon. Is that richt?' She had him floundering and unprepared for a sudden belligerent swerve. 'Bit,' she scowled and the blue eyes became slits, 'dinnae think ye can come here an' tell us fit tae dae! It maks nae odds ava': yon fence wis richt eneuch afore yir bull brak through't. Ye'll get deil aa oot o' me mister, a'll nae pey oot siller on your say-so!'

It was time to go. Whether or not the whisky had just hit her he was back more or less where he started, at knife point. Again, how the hell did Ron Fox cope? When he thanked her for the drinks he felt like the smooth sod she thought he was. Following as he strode to the door he imagined her dealing with a tink or burglar. Even now she was capable of inflicting GBH. Never again could he believe in dear old ladies.

With a final glare he was wafted into the darkening afternoon to make way along the faint track. Stepping over the boundary fence he began to sing to recover his spirits; he had achieved nothing, was no further forrard, would have to do the blasted fence himself, she would never let Fox. The whisky hazed him enough to make his wavering baritone sound rather pleasant as it rolled over the gathering dusk. Bewildered old ewes scuttled to a safe distance. He carried no food and was making unfamiliar noises. They stared after him for some time before resuming a listless search for a tasty bite in the spent grass.

'...how sweet you are ... how sweet, hahow sweet yoohoo are. Thou once wa ... as lost a ... an now art found ... was lost and now art found...' He knew, if the ewes did not, he hadn't got the words quite right.

Over the mantelshelf in that marvellous room there was a photograph in faded sepia of a girl on a horse, a big girl on a big horse; it must have been Hannah. He could picture her in this sort of light making for home, strong and proud, an Amazon. That face before age got to it. And was the mouth different, not so mean? He continued with 'A-hamazi-ing Grace' but stopped when he saw lights from his house powering out the beacon Charlotte loved to send for his benefit, for the general good and that of the Hydro Board. She would have to be told!

12

'There were giants in the earth in those days...'

There was endless work as the weather eased: roofs had gaping holes, fences were down and walls tumbled, roads needed repair; all this and the many routines in preparation for planting. It was time also for alterations or new building to go ahead.

Little time then for less serious things like forming a team for the tug-of-war. Unlike young men in Aberdeen who went to health clubs to shape up, the farmers' sons had all the exercise they needed and after their labours the pub was more to their taste. Rarely did the same ones turn up at Burnside and John understood. Busy himself and tired out, he would have followed suit had the pub been nearer. With heavier built lads unfortunately the tendency led to thickening waists and the beginnings of pot bellies, but the summer deadline, the agricultural show, seemed a long way off.

He was taking the only information he could gather about tug-of-war from a book dated 1903, which Charlotte found very funny. 'What about bare-knuckle fighters John? It says here John L. Sullivan was an outstanding champion. That might catch on!' She got a withering look.

One evening some of the men were waiting for others to turn up when they saw the temporary repair John had made to the damaged march fence. One look and the idea of pulling at a rope seemed a waste of time.

'We'll gie ye a haun' John wi' yon. Git yir pinch an' the piky wire.' Nobody could have faulted the way they tackled the job. They queried as the repair took shape, 'This een's surely a march fence John? Nae yir fence ava' the wye it is! Yon's a pawky chiel, maist likely 'e thinks ye winna ken.'

'Fit wye did the bugger pit the beast theer on bare grun an' sic like? Nivver richt, afore yon fence wis sorted.'

'It's nae his bull onywye, 'e's jis' luikin' efter it.'

'Some bluidy wye o' daein' that!'

This support made John wish to do really well for the team, coach them to a little glory, however fleeting. He tried to fix the best places for men who managed to turn up regularly while remembering the weight and strengths of some who came less often but were keen enough. There was a worrying lack of bulk: only a cheerful lad called Tom had any great size. He was more than six feet tall with enormous shoulders and great muscular arms and thighs, the obvious anchorman. The trouble was a tapering down to a whippet of a man Tom proved he could lift with one hand. The in-between sizes, though strong and used to hard graft, tended to have the variable waistlines.

Employed on a farm not too far away if you cut across the fields, Tom came most times. He enjoyed the suppers Charlotte provided. John wished they would all eat like him and get more bulk. Charlotte, watching her baking disappear at a rate of knots into Tom's great maw, was not so sure. She was mollified on hearing he had said: 'Yir missus is a michty fine haun' wi' the pastry John, an' nivver did I taste sic' a fine sponge loaf!' Good old Aga. Credit where credit was due.

Once you have seen one agricultural show you have seen them all. This in the Howe, small though it was, lacked nothing. A fine nostalgic scent from the newly-cut field interlaced that from animals, flowers, food, cigars, beer and frying onions – and people.

John watched cattle get a final grooming before a parade in front of the judges. The preferences and prejudices of these men were well known in the Howe and the decisions they came to were likely to be discussed and questioned long after the day was ended. It was a pleasure to see beasts so quiet, used to the halter, unfazed by the crowds; rarely did a polished hoof stamp or an immaculate cleaned tail give a flick of protest. Many were the signs of perfect health: a sheen on the coat, a bright alert eye, good stance. His own animals were healthy but even Lucy, whom he sometimes called 'my dove', did not compare with this mild-mannered élite. He thought of Gertie, suspicious if you offered a friendly hand to sniff. You would get the horn if you tried anything fancy with her. He turned to Charlotte.

'What do you think? Like to go in for showing? Must take a lot of time, but they do look good.'

She took a long look at the cattle and the people still titivating them minutes before the parade. 'I wouldn't John, couldn't im-agine... They are super, deserve all the glory

120

and the prizes, but I prefer ones like ours, wildish.' She pointed to a cow who had dared to defecate standing patiently for a rapid clean-up, 'I reckon our Gertie might learn a lot from that one!'

They moved off, keeping an eye open for any of the team, though tug-of-war was the last item on the programme. John wanted to confirm all had hammered steel studs into their boot soles as he suggested. If not, spares were in the Land Rover. The grass certainly appeared slippery after rain in the night.

It was a pleasant day with a slight breeze coming from the hills, better for the animals than excessive heat. Casually dressed people ambled round looking at the exhibits: young parents wanting to show their children something different; a few tourists, French or Germans, their clothes having a slight difference which drew the eye; Americans, genial and polite, open to everything Scottish; elderly people in well-cut but worn tweeds; and also in the Howe the kilt was rig of the day, its wearer inured to stares. Dressed up a bit for the occasion local people took the chance to chat, catch up on gossip, a genuine change for wives from isolated farms. Charlotte recognised one or two faces but could not put names to them. They walked along and now and again words drifted across making them smile: 'English'; 'Burnside'; 'London'. It was recognition in its way.

But a shock was in store: Charlotte lingered to look at hand-knitted sweaters displayed by the WRI, the 'Rural' as it was known, and turning to catch up with John collided with ... a giant? About seven feet tall, dressed in a coverall, something embroidered on the pocket; boots slung round his neck, giant's boots, the soles bristling with steel spikes! It couldn't be, could it? She found John who had seen the giant and was gazing after him with something akin to horror. They walked rapidly, searching for more giants and were unfortunate enough to find a lot. It seemed busloads from Brobdingnag had just arrived: not only clones in red but different ones in blue and green and grey, some knotting the laces of spiky boots to hang at the neck like the first giant. All seemed to have cheerful smiles. Maybe another requirement like being very tall indeed and having size 14 feet.

Nearby, a raised platform with plenty of seats in front and at the sides; people to watch you, your hair in a wee bun atop your head, a blouse white and frilled, a mini-kilt, long socks and dancing feet needing only ... someone to squeeze the accordion and free the bouncing notes and then you could spring high but neatly and narrowly down if you were well taught, and the tartan pleats would flare and twirl! Marvellous to be a little girl or a rather bigger one for the dance was open to different ages and even boys could enter; silver buckles to their shoes and all, but the littlest girls were best, got most applause ... had the secret smiles tucked at the corner of their mouths.

A powerful draw to someone like Charlotte but the charm must be resisted, the Burnside men had to be found and warned. They were outside the beer tent talking to Tom, a single look revealing he had spent some time inside that place, but all were downcast, did not need telling, were aware of the envoys from outer space. It was decided that far from throwing in the sponge or towel, or committing suicide or emigrating, the team would, like men, stay and fight, wavering only when they learned their opponents were the 'reds', victors at English shows, and apparently in Holland, France and Germany, the champions of

Europe, no less! It was something to wonder at, fate beckoning such gods to this particular place, hardly 'Field of the Cloth of Gold', the Howe.

Time before the encounter to get some tea and take a stroll round the marquees: small animals, caged birds, flower arrangements, vegetables, needlework, home baking. And the competitors, it was easy to spot those daring enough. Amongst casual onlookers were people with down-turned mouths, with wry faces, comparing, disparaging. A mere few stayed close to the rosettes taking pleasure from congratulations, some sincere. People with no taste for the spillage of dislike and envy which can be the aftermath of challenge are not persuaded to enter competitions like this. Charlotte refused when it was suggested, but was secretly pleased to note her stuff bore comparison. She did not expect to waver even when things were more settled: after all it was supposed to be fun, not a fight to the death. Which also could be said about the tug-of-war.

Better really to draw a veil over the event at 'cinco de la tarde', as bullfighters know the hour of five o'clock in the afternoon. The show was considered important enough for the BBC to send a popular celebrity as master of ceremonies, a civil man and very competent. Beforehand he quizzed the champions' coach and John Grey for details which would interest the crowd, anything they thought relevant: for John, racking his brains, this amounted to very little except the names of his warriors. When Archie took up the microphone the BBC voice like a chameleon slipped into the colourful shades of the Doric.

'Weel folks, noo the grandest thing in the hale programme o' this fine agricultural event, a gran' treat for us a' the day an' the climax o' the show, the tug-of-war!' He gave it the emphasis of Noah launching the ark or sighting land. Riding the cheers and boos and laughter of the crowd he grabbed the large trophy to be won and held it aloft. 'This muckle siller cup, an' fit a bonnie thing, wis donated langsyne by nane ither than His Grace, the Marquess o' Aiberdeen, no less! The Marquess o' Aiberdeen! Noo I dinna ken if that great gentleman ivver wid tak a pu' at the rope in his ain time? Bit we hiv folks tae warsle awa' wi'et an' they'll dae jis' that.' He put down the cup and beckoned the teams. 'We hiv a team frae this neiperhuid, oor very ain team coached by Mr Grey, Mr John Grey that is, weel ken't in these parts.' A small cheer because he was not, people obviously wondering, who? 'An a team frae England.' Boos and cheers and whistles. 'A team frae that country I mentioned, wha' carried a' thing afore them at hame and whiles wint on tae knock sivin bells oot o' the Continentals.' He burbled on while the champions of Europe won the toss and chose to station themselves with backs to the sun.

'These mannies mak' a braw sicht tae my thinkin, buskit in sic' bonnie reid suits wi' thir names in gowd on thir pooch at the tap. A'body'll be spikkin' aboot that!'

John led Tom and the lesser men to their end of the rope to squint into an oddly powerful sun. 'An noo Mr Grey an' friens fae the slopes of Lochnagar. Mr Grey wha mak's a fair job o' breedin knout awa' up theer an' he's got taegither a fine body o' men also, an' lat me see...' he paused, Tom's red face above a flowery shirt the only thing to notice, the rest ordinary beyond description. His eyes flickered towards the looming giants, magnificent, still smiling, waiting to make the kill. Hastily he resumed, 'Mr Grey's team, folks, are wearin...' and triumphing over the odds he ended, 'thir a' wearin' thir ain cleise!'

13

'If you can dream...'

A pure-bred Aberdeen Angus cow, Eva-Jan (sire: Ferguson-Pirate) was of special significance for John Grey. She cost twice the price of any other cow, in fact she was his 'luxury' and also a bit of a gamble.

Originally he had the idea of a pedigree herd but realising it was impractical, even naive, to think of entering such a specialised world, he settled for crossbred cows. Bowing to this expedient he still wanted first-class animals, so went to a breeder of high repute and was offered big solid-rumped, deep-chested cows, all with growthy calves at foot. There was no doubt as to the quality of the ones he bought, and he became very proud of them, but love of the Angus breed did not go away. To the embarrassment of his wife in a supermarket he was likely to stand in front of displays of beef and in his good strong voice remark, 'Flavourless that'll be,' pointing at some pallid joint. 'Taste like cardboard!' Or, seeing someone lift a pack of pinkish characterless steak, 'How people buy stuff like that!' Charlotte, seeing the look on his pleasant face with its robust air of health would try to pull him away before too many suppers were spoiled or sales plummeted.

When the *Press & Journal* reported that George Ferguson was retiring from farming and the cattle to be sold included a batch of purebred Angus cows, it was natural for John to send for a catalogue of sale. Studying this prompted visits to the Ferguson farm near Inverness, and to the sale. He came back with Eva-Jan and her calf, five-month old Emma-Jan.

Charlotte of course loved them on sight, though she admitted not minding about breed or pedigree as long as a cow was not wild and difficult like some she could name. Alastair was the one who suggested the 'luxury' tag and ribbed John for being a romantic. John rose to the bait and mounted his hobby-horse.

'What the heck's romantic about wanting to produce the best possible beef? Something juicy and tender? With a taste to it? Good eating as opposed to dried cardboard? Tell me the last time you ate a real steak Alastair!'

'A steak? On my salary? You've gotta' be joking!'

'It's your own fault, all you Scots! You have this cow traditionally producing the best beef in the whole world and you dump her because she's not a giant, costs little to feed and gives birth easily, or you spoil her by putting her to a bloody great giant from the Continent, nearly killing her in the process!'

Alastair rooted for his pipe in the pocket of the Barbour he wore for visits to the farms. This coat remained a townsman's coat, stiffish and clean, lacking the slightly ripe odours of John's similar one. Tamping down the baccy in the bowl and getting it alight took a time and offered a screen for his thoughts.

'It's a funny ole' world!' he said. He did admire Eva-Jan when he saw her and thought Emma-Jan a great calf – a 'topper', to use the favourite word. In due course this little heifer would join others bought from Carnegie.

Now the mother was 'fairing' to calve again. John determined to be on hand: in no way could he risk being absent from any birth but this meant more than looking after a cow or adding to the herd. His 'luxury' of course, she was also the symbol of what he truly believed, an example of 'putting your money where your mouth is', something of that sort.

As he waited not too close to the cow, as he had learned, he remembered George Ferguson and the day of the sale. He had spoken to the elderly man of good, almost military, bearing, precisely dressed, well-cut tweed jacket, a Tattersall shirt, fine pullover, knee-breeches and thick socks, Trickers' shoes highly polished not at risk on the swept and cleaned concrete of his yard. John, intent on his own affairs, did not often see as Charlotte did what might lie behind the face presented to the world, but in this instance it was obvious. There was pain and regret in the eyes of the man, and he had difficulty in maintaining a stoic appearance. He tried to make light of it. 'Better go down the road before they have to carry me Mr? Mr Grey,' as John supplied his name. He went on, 'I'm damned if I want to part with my farm, but my sons are not interested, educated too highly by a fool of a father! I suppose I wanted to give them the chances I never had. Anyway, they both live abroad making more money than I ever did and I'm considered successful! Being tied to a cow's tail is not their idea of a good life. But I must not dwell on what might have been, rots a fellow that! Tell me what brings you, an Englishman I think, to this part of the world?'

They talked for a while before one of the farm men came for final instructions, the sale half an hour away from starting. It was the end of a lifetime's work as their beauties were brought to parade in front of the auctioneer. Master and men watched with the same sad air about them.

Bidding reflected the excitement and interest in this sale; people had come from far afield drawn by the reputation of the breeder. Neighbours and local farmers were all there. One by one the fine animals were led out.

Cynics theorise about farmers, suggesting a streak of atavism likely to surface when animals are marketed. A farmer might be mean to his wife, deny her spending-money, or a new kitchen; never would his children have the sort of toys their schoolmates took for granted; gallivanting abroad was very unlikely for his family. Yet this man, this same man, if an animal at the mart or at a roup should take his fancy no matter the size of his overdraft or his strained relations with the 'banker' would throw his bonnet into the ring and he would bid and bid.

John edged his way to the front to get a clear view and waited until it was the turn of the Angus cows, all with calves at foot. He knew which one he preferred but feared she might fetch too much money. Eventually his choice was sent out, calf bonded as if glued to her side and the bids mounted rapidly. John kept silent until interest slackened, the chosen time for his own bid. As expected more was offered but then a new voice interrupted – did someone have the same strategy as himself? His first opponent gave up; the new one continued increasing the amount in a determined way until John, at the outside limit of what he could spend, was left the victor and owner of cow and calf. Looking round trying to identify other bidders his eyes met those of a man from land adjoining Burnside: a wry lift of the shoulders acknowledged defeat. John responded with a straight look, suspecting slyness in the smiling face. Afterwards he wondered if the beggar had been 'upping' him, not serious except to make John pay more. Even now he was not sure after all the gossip in the beginning, the 'fowk fae Lunnon' stuff and him 'needin' his head examin't', the blighters always seemed to witness anything he did

132

particularly when he made a cock-up.

But that was in the past. Now he murmured to Eva-Jan: 'Well lassie, we'll have to show 'em won't we? You give me a real beauty of a heifer, eh?' There was not much sign yet, she was fussing about, restless, moving away and then returning to the same spot, tail lashing, not quite ready for the second more intensive stage. He was wondering whether to go back to the house for a quick snack when he saw Charlotte climbing towards him carrying food and flasks of tea and coffee.

'Have you told Eva-Jan we need a heifer calf?' she asked, handing him a massive sandwich.

The weather was lovely: wisps of white cloud hovered against a high blue ceiling, the sun coaxing out all the good smells of earth, grass, flowers. The 'bonny days'.

'Before you came I was thinking of the sale,' John said. 'How Ron Fox started bidding against me and whether he really wanted her.'

'He *is* quite fox-like, thinking of that sandy hair and pointed smile and,' wickedly, 'he does use a very strong aftershave. Which came first I wonder, the sly look, or were his forbears so sly they got the name?'

'Another of your fascinating speculations! I know I don't trust the beggar!' Eva-Jan took his attention. 'It looks as if she's getting down to it.'

There seemed to be no complications, the cow had read the books; two black hooves, clearly front feet, and soon a glimpse of tongue. Intense effort, totally focused, heedless of the silent watchers, of sun, sky or scented earth. Accelerating violent strains, a rest to gather all strength and then in an immense groaning completion a calf slithering and twitching on the grass. A suffocating caul to be torn away and thick mucus from its spluttering jaws. John having to step back to avoid a sharp nudge from Eva-Jan, in no mood to have her calf touched: it looked very much like a heifer.

'Clever girl!' Charlotte could only whisper, always overwhelmed by this moment.

The calf's head, seemingly too heavy for its thin stalk of a neck, wavered and blindly lifted, a black nose wrinkled, sampling air. Under a barrage of frantic licking a voice was discovered to bleat protest. Tiny hooves made of something incredibly new and perfect ended spindly legs being bravely tested until they could coordinate and make a stand. Eventually guided by instinct, the mother's tender noises and her gently thrusting head, the calf stumbled against the udder to find a teat. A tentative mouth becoming sure as rich milk came, a tail lashing pleasure against a tiny still-wet rump. Listening to strong sucking it was impossible not to smile.

'A heifer John, just as you hoped.'

A smile and a gentle touch on Eva-Jan's wary nose and then, 'I'm going to ring old Ferguson and tell him. I know he'll be interested.'

'What about ringing old Foxy as well?'

'Take care, madam, if you want some champagne!'

In a long overdue letter after ordinary exchanges Charlotte wrote:

We have a beautiful heifer calf from the pedigree cow, that makes three, a start anyway. She is rather special, the mother I mean, represents for John:

(1) The first time he bought at a roup (auction) and backed his own judgement.

(2) The first time he drove the LR with a horse-box attached.

Both traumatic. Re. (2) John drove along knowing he could not reverse – incredibly different with a trailer – it was a maze of narrow roads so if he found himself on the wrong one he would have to go on and on ('Travels with an Expensive Cow' to rival RLS's Donkey?).

Another thing happened on the way home. Pulling up at traffic lights there was suddenly a tremendous crash: John flew out, imagining the cow broken loose somehow and off into the blue with the calf, then a desperate chase like on TV. *But* the door was still fastened, the cow safe inside. The crash had come from a great load of rubble dropped from scaffolding on a building at the junction! John looked up to see workmen grinning and shouting what sounded like 'That fairly pit the wind up ye, Jimmy!'

It sure did.

Much love, C.

Charlotte did not write about the furious beeping John had to put up with when the light turned green or the identity of the 'beeper', giving a cheeky wave as he overtook before John could get started again.

14

'So that's what hay looks like...'

Queen Mary had been very surprised when she saw hay for the first time. If John and Charlotte drove anywhere in the Howe and saw hay being turned, or in neat windrows ready for the baler, or stacked for carting off the field, it exercised a pressure on John to make a start, get going, though his grass was not ready for cutting. Like the melting of snow-cover on a high farm, ripening of any crop was always 'later'.

His first year's hay was good because it was an excellent summer. This second would be more of a test if you took the view that good summers, particularly over the border, rarely strike twice. At the time he had been very much the 'new boy', easy and agreeable, willing to make allowances and put up with delays if sound reasons were given. Not any more! Contractors were in for a shock if they had him written down as a pushover! Last year it was civilly, 'Will you manage today?', or 'What happened?' The answer, on the lines of, 'Weel there's jis' this sivin acre tae cut, an'anither fower bit ah've nae forgotten, will see ye, cheerio jis' noo!' All with the best of intentions whilst the fields waited.

Some contractors were of good repute, others not. John now knew one or two farmers who worked on other people's hay as a sideline to earn extra cash and help pay for their own machinery. Official or un-official, all were the same when it came to promises and only if the weatherman could offer long sunny days with the right amout of wind would all be fulfilled. In any event, John was prepared and did not care a hoot what impression he made. All that mattered was getting the hay cut, baled or carted when he wanted, not after every other beggar was given first call. He intended to fight to get it right; if firm talk was necessary, well he hadn't been in the Service for nothing, he knew the language!

He had seen a lot of weather around the world, had experienced the short moun-tainous seas of the Arctic and below zero temperatures followed once by orders to proceed without delay down the Denmark Strait with its icebergs to the Bay of Biscay and then Gibraltar, the rough and the smooth as it were, though contrary to most people's beliefs the blue Mediterranean could offer up some pretty rough stuff in the way of sudden storms. Weather had been all-important then but he had not quite grasped that as a farmer it would still occupy his waking thoughts, be so vital, govern success or failure in so many aspects of the new way of life.

Grass cut at the right stage of growth, green but just on the point of maturing, cloudless skies with sun and light winds for turning and baling, hay-bales left in the field to 'finish' before carting and stacking. Contractors punctually on the farm, no machinery breakdowns, such is the hay of dreams or of Cloud Cuckoo Land. A shower of rain in the early stages of making hay is not too serious, but if tossing and turning has brought grass to perfection, and it is ready, dry and sweet-smelling and the machine with only a minor adjustment has made long rows of even swathes, airy and high on the greening field, let rain fall then, not in showers but pouring from a black-ened sky and you have disaster.

Only brilliant sun and a fair wind can dry sodden twisted grass spread out over the whole field for work to begin all over again, and a long time will elapse before bales can be made. Sadly the quality of these bales has gone, which matters more than the double cost of producing them. It does not do to think of the way any farmer feels.

'How do people stand it?' Charlotte had been appalled watching beautiful swathes flatten in Joe's fields below them. Gilbert was also at the window seeing their neighbour's work come to nothing: he was uncompromising.

'His ain fault! We've all gotten oors. He's ivver late, jis' will not get going.'

John, agreeing, still tried to be charitable. 'He's got the idea probably from what he was told as a lad that there's more body in the hay if he leaves it; doesn't hold with what he called 'modren' thinking, cutting greenish, prefers bulk, he told me.'

Gilbert, knowing more than they did, was brutal: 'That family suffers from the serious complaint o' being bone idle, an' it goes weel back intae history that! They're aye behint the times and they learn nothin'. Don't be fooled by a' the flummery John.' His father's barns were overflowing with high quality bales taken at the right time and by long hours of intensive work.

'I saw Joe and his son this morning,'

140

Charlotte broke in, frowning. 'It was odd they seemed just as usual, Joe a bit well, smarmy and the son unforthcoming. But not down in the dumps as we would be, just...' She could not put into words how indifferent they seemed, how unaffected by what she felt was shattering. 'If it were me or us I would be out there flailing my fists, calling on Heaven, screaming and shouting words I've heard John use, going absolutely mad.'

'Make a note Gil,' John mused, 'I remember poor old Charley!'

'I would like fine tae witness that ma'am.' Gilbert's tanned face showed a wicked grin. 'When next it rains!'

There was one incident in John's introduction to hay-making which he preferred to forget, except that it still made him and Charlotte laugh if reminded of it. A finger-bar mower, a rather primitive appliance bought in a first flush of enthusiasm for farm implements for the sum of £60 figured in this. John planned to contract out farm operations which needed expensive machinery, considering it uneconomic for him to tie up money that could be put to better use buying stock. For the most part George Orwell's 'Four legs good, two legs bad'

141

became 'Four legs good, four wheels bad', but the finger-bar mower was a minor deviation, merely a small attachment to mount on a tractor which might just save a little money if it would slice thistles off the permanent pasture or maybe cut a small field of grass.

Learning to drive a tractor had not been a worry: John got hold of an instruction manual and practised behind the buildings out of sight from neighbours. The finger-mower had no manual and after attaching it to the three-point linkage he decided to make use of expert knowledge. A charming chap from the Agricultural Training Board was quick to offer help when telephoned; he would send someone along.

Jim James looked like a prosperous farmer, well dressed in a checked tweed jacket and light trousers, neat shirt and tie, well-polished shoes. Stocky and cheerful he had a vigorous air about him and got down to business at once. The first thing was to have the blades sharp otherwise you could not function. Next you mowed the 'lands', a few strips at the top and bottom of your field or 'park' as he termed it, to give you ample room to make the turn as you mowed up and down. He demonstrated and it seemed simple enough to John: the bar was down on the grass for cutting, then a lever pulled to raise it at the turn so you kept a continuous movement. Down to the bottom of the park cutting, pull, swing round, lever back to cutting, up the length of the park cutting, pull, swing again and so on.

John took over the driving but went too slowly so the cutting stopped because the blades fouled up and had to be cleared with everything switched off for safety. Jim was really emphatic about safety. The second attempt was successful, good straight swathes made on upward and downward runs. Jim dropped off when the tractor next reached the top of the park and removed his coat as the day had turned hot. Used to driving an Alfa-Romeo John had never been a slouch behind a wheel; apart from a couple of stops where the ground was bumpy he made rapid progress. The thought occurred that on any other than this sparse field, say one with grass in great abundance, the blades would clog up more often and it would mean hopping in and out of the tractor time after time and be extremely tiring. Still it was pleasant cruising up and down and whizzing round at the, ends. It was very hot. Jim had settled himself in the shade of an old sycamore at the top corner, nice work if you can get it, better than working for a living! The cutting seemed right enough though there was an awful lot of field left. Turnabout was becoming automatic and, like Jim, John could do it at speed now. Perhaps that last one a bit fast, he may have accelerated too much. In the mirror he saw Jim had left the shade and was waving, probably deciding to push off now John had the hang of it. He made a satisfying swift turn at the bottom and trundled up towards the instructor.

Jim had not been 'just waving' to say goodbye. His face was red and angry, each hand brandished a piece of what used to be a good tweed jacket! The last turn at the top had been not only too fast but a helluva sight too close to the fence!

What was there to say? John resisted an impulse to scold, 'You should not leave your clothes lying around,' as Charlotte was apt to tell him. He well knew his humour leaned towards the macabre, so with a tremendous effort stifled an offer to 'distress' Jim's trousers to make a matching suit of it. He felt his face go red and hoped Jim would think it was the flush of shame.

After the car left with a stony-faced Jim at

the wheel, John kept on at the mowing. Down the park, swing, up, swing, somehow the joy had gone out of it. Completing the cut took a long, long time. He climbed stiffly out of the cab and went to tell his wife. Her eyes were wide with dismay. 'You say ruined, completely? Could I have...?' When he shook his head emphatically she resolved, 'We must pay for it. Buy him another. Hope he isn't a Gieves' man.' She tried to read a rather enigmatic look on John's face to no avail. He was going to wait before he told her about the matching suit. 'Well, what did he say then? However did he take what you did?'

A long pause and then carefully, 'Nothing much really. I wouldn't say he was er, overjoyed!'

Ignoring the bent towards jacket-slicing the finger-bar mower could not deal with any lush crop and was relegated to use for thistles only. A few people borrowed it for that and eventually it disappeared.

15

'Haud fast...'

Traditionally the farm fields had names to identify them – for example, West Top, Middle West, and Low West were three fields bordering the hill. Some names related to places near them, like High Blairs or Low Blairs, some to landmarks in a field such as Old Mill or Wellhouse. John and Charlotte frivolously changed 'Sycamore', the one where the dervish finger mower had its debut, to 'Jacket'. One very beautiful part at the southern end of the farm had been a separate holding, its name (Craigie Step) printed on the Ordnance Survey map, though Joe Waddell's mother remembered it as Teuchatshoose, translated as 'House of the Lapwings'.

An avenue of matured Geans led up to the ruins of this croft house and its tiny garden. On a summer evening strolling to look at the cows, the new heifers and Charley the 'quiet' bull, it was pleasant to linger, trying to visualise the past. Mrs Waddell spoke of ten children trooping off to a school no longer there, all neat and clean, carrying little bags with probably a 'jeely piece' for lunch. Now weeds were rampant over the tumbled stones while one or two bushes had survived somehow, to give a little fruit which birds took. Not much of pride, except when, shading from vivid pink paler and paler to pure white, masses of wild roses scented the dusks of late June.

Animals did well at Craigie Step, seeking out 'natural' grasses on the high slopes in preference to a reseeded lower part. There were sights to enchant – sleeping calves in the old ruined house, one aloft on the broad sill of a window, its head at a quizzical angle against an upright of pink granite; a cow keeping guard, blinking as a spray of blossom vanished down her wide throat. Elysium.

Yet this was the scene of a freak accident, long lasting in its effect on them all. It occurred after very heavy rain fell throughout one day, the whole of the night and the next day. Swathed in oilskins, patrolling perhaps a little later than usual, John had found it difficult to make a count, with animals widely spread at the top of the park among the ruins or huddled under the shelter of the leafy Geans, where their feet trampled layer upon layer of fallen white petals. A wrong number could be a mistake in counting or trouble ahead. Wearisome at any time to start the round again, in such conditions it was tempting to give up and hope for the best.

He discovered the calf, black with a white face and patchy white and black inside the ears, a little heifer clumsily named 'Chalky-lugs' by a child present at its birth. Like a carcass at a butcher's shop poor 'Chalky' was hanging upside-down over a crumbling wall which originally shored up the avenue of trees, her hind legs trapped under thick exposed roots slippery with moss. John tried hard to free her and failed: struggling had probably made things worse, entangling her more surely in the twisted roots. The poor creature was alive but only just, suspended with nose not quite touching the ground for hour after hour, perhaps throughout the night whilst he and Charlotte slept. Stones from the wall were too firmly embedded to shift as a support for the head. There was nothing else, he had to go back...

Cursing his clumsy oilskins he ran uphill to the house to alert Charlotte and get tools from the steading. For once she had not dressed, was in pyjamas and dressing gown preparing breakfast for his return. She quickly got into oilskins and ran to follow. A bow saw for the thick roots and sacks to protect the calf, a heavy axe and a bale of straw; all went into the back of the Land Rover. At speed they got as near as possible to the top of the park and rushed over to the tree. Charlotte was dismayed at the sight, and tried as John had to find a way to untangle the feet but it had to be the saw. Carefully John packed sacking round the legs while she crouched, managing to support the head a little. The saw slipped and slithered before the teeth got hold. Completed, the cut made no difference. John tackled the next root and the next until all were sawn through. Together they tried to ease the calf away but the feet remained tightly held.

The problem was that the calf's weight, of about three hundredweights, made it impossible to lift her to ease the concentrated downward pressure on her hocks. John dared not make cuts closer to the legs. After anxious thought and almost as a last resort he used the axe handle to prize the cuts so far apart that the weight shifted and Chalky was free, an inert muddied heap on the ground. It had taken more than half an hour. Cows clustering round when the rescue started had lost interest and moved off; the mother only a short distance away snatching an occasional mouthful of grass but making no attempt to come near. The rain showed no sign of stopping.

Charlotte climbed into the Land Rover. 'I'll get the vet then?'

John answered slowly. 'Yes, it's no good moving her when we can't assess the damage, only a vet would have the know-how, but it doesn't look so good, I'd say.' He made an effort to be practical. 'Ring him, then fetch more straw and the pinch, you know the thing I use for digging holes for a fence? It's in the tool place.'

She released the brake and pulled away, sliding and bouncing, going too fast across such ground; a check before lurching towards the gateway then the noise of brakes as she slewed smartly into the road – Stirling Moss couldn't have managed better. The thought did little to cheer John as he waited beside the calf in a landscape of obliterating rain and mud and sadness. To combat the chill settling on his bones he began trying to loosen stones which prevented a vehicle getting close to the calf. Charlotte came back with more sacking and straw to edge beneath and round Chalky, and an oilskin as a cover, though wetness mattered little now. They both struggled with stones until at last the vet's car appeared on the farm road.

'I'll get him!' John was away, the Land Rover not flamboyant but faster under his hands. The vet seemed incredibly dry in a coverall made of fine waterproof material neatly fitted at throat and ankles. He wore expensive-looking short boots. As if in sympathy with elegance and suitability, the rain eased. Charlotte felt suddenly conscious of the pyjamas beneath her oilskins and her feet so cold and bare in muddy wellies. The verdict was brief.

'The knacker man's your best bet I think! I'd be inclined to cut my losses if I were you!'

'What about moving her? The legs? Are they broken anywhere? Obviously you can't tell about anything internal.'

'Badly bruised I'd say, and damaged, but nothing broken as far as I can see. To be fair I can't see this beast making out in the long run even if it survives. It's entirely your decision of course.'

'Yes. It is, isn't it?' Without reason John

disliked this man. 'Now, can you wait till I get the buckrake?' An unwilling glance at the wrist. The watch expensive too. 'I suppose so, if you're quick.'

The three of them manoeuvred the calf onto the buckrake, securing it as best they could with thin rope from the Land Rover. As John lifted the implement and set off down the field it triggered a reaction from the cow forgotten until then. No longer keeping a watchful distance, she ran after the machine, bawling as if anguished. The vet climbed neatly into the Land Rover and Charlotte drove off not too closely behind the cow, ready to stop if she turned – essential to have her with the calf. John at the gateway felt the buckrake sway wildly as the tractor slithered in deep mud but somehow their makeshift fastening held and he was on a better surface with only a short distance to go.

'Will you come up?' Charlotte asked the vet, when the cow was also through and she could follow. 'You can turn more easily on the close.' She really wanted him to look again at the calf but did not want to hear another no-hope verdict. She got down to shut the field gate on cows willing to stream up into the shelter of the steading, given the chance.

John had driven into the court and was making a thick bed of straw in one corner; he had given the cow a wedge of hay which she was munching at the trough, as if back in familiar surroundings and out of the never-ending rain all would be well. It was far from that. The vet helped to move the calf onto the straw.

'I'll give her a jab of antibiotic now.' He was expert, syringe filled, needle inserted, withdrawn: no reaction from the calf.

Charlotte had returned to the house to shed the dripping oilskins and boots; her pyjamas were wet and muddy and she realised how cold she felt. It took minutes under the hot shower before she could control the shivering. Dressing rapidly in slacks and a warm sweater she went back to the kitchen. As usual the coffee pot was on the Aga. She placed mugs and a plate of biscuits on a tray and lingered with hands over the hotplate's shiny top. When they came in she suggested John should dry off and get into warm clothes, indicating the bathroom for the vet to wash his hands.

Drinking the steaming coffee, Ian Scott no longer seemed in a hurry, was glancing around at the dresser with its colourful plates and dishes, the beautiful old table set for a breakfast never taken, the fine clock ticking a measured note. He decided to be frank.

'Do you realise there's a fair amount of speculation about you two? People wonder, I myself do, what motivated you? After all you won't expect a fortune from a few suckler cows. You must surely have income from other sources, private means?' His voice tailed off at the look on Charlotte's face. She felt angry at such impertinence, he deserved a snub but she managed to hold back.

'How very amusing!' she said without smiling, 'I do think people are perhaps less concerned than you think, particularly when you are there.' She had heard this man was a snob; they said he kept a special outfit in case he was called to Balmoral to treat anything royal. She continued easily. 'When you see them, their animals sick perhaps "even unto death", surely people are thinking of their own affairs rather than ours?' She put careful emphasis on the words, her voice light and superficial, reminiscent of her friend Lisa making some sort of social point, politely rude. She looked at his face, it was sharp with reddened skin over the cheekbones; he had a vain little moustache

154

above a small pursed mouth. He did not fit as a ministering angel.

'May I offer you more coffee?' she asked, 'or are you anxious to be away?' He was gone before John claimed his coffee but in a way left his mark: Charlotte found it, a muddy footprint in the centre of the white bathroom rug John had always declared unsuitable for a farm.

The calf was the main concern, alive but totally inert. Charlotte tried to clean her up but in such a sorry state it seemed better not to fuss. They packed more straw round her and left. Later they found the cow taking up most of the bedding, contented and cudding away. The calf must have felt comfort and warmth from the nearness of the mother, a benefit impossible to assess for any young thing. Next morning they were cheered to see an improvement, eyes well opened, the chequered ears no longer drooping. In the afternoon, head up, she was certainly aware of the mother, again lying comfortably alongside. John was prepared to strip the cow of surplus milk but she appeared in no discomfort. He could not clearly see the udder because of the way she was lying and had to disturb her to get a close look. The teats showed no distension or soreness and looked normal, making him wonder if by some miracle the calf had sucked.

It was true. Charlotte, going regularly to check, found the cow managing to place herself over the calf exactly where the poor weak head could reach to suck. It was a touching and pitiful sight, the big lumbering body so delicately poised over the small helpless one. How wrong they had been thinking she had given up on the calf. She had followed the Land Rover but once in the court spent most of the time eating at the trough, not going near it. Biding her time? Waiting for them to go? Did a thinking process go on in that head or was it instinct, blind mothering instinct? Whatever it was she, Mary the cow, was going to get a 'puckle' of those expensive cow cobs the herd found so tasty. With a lighter heart Charlotte went to tell John the news.

The work of the farm went on. Charlotte helped where she could and took total responsibility for Chalky. The little creature was very appealing, framed in the nest of straw, head up, eyes bright, ears alert, though not a sign of body movement. Which was a worry. However, she was feeding normally from the cow and nibbling the hay and grass Charlotte scythed. Because Mary helped herself too freely from Chalky's rations and really needed to graze she was allowed to go on the hill with the old ewes and their lambs, but never failed to return to suckle and sleep beside her calf.

For a while this was the pattern until the herd moved back up to Jacket. Seeing and hearing them was too much – Mary would stand at the highest point of the hill and bawl at them. Knowing she would probably get a fierce buffeting if kept out too long, John opened the gate for her. Without much trouble she regained her place in the bunt and was allowed to settle. It meant Charlotte fetching her twice a day to suckle Chalky. Mostly she cooperated, was willing, even anxious, to be extracted. In time she took to waiting at the gate when ready. It was worth the trouble, and became routine, the cow kept healthy and content, the calf not able to move but looking better every day.

It went on for weeks like this. Charlotte took to grooming Chalky like a show animal and was indignant when the vet said it was useless. The man seemed unable to see why they could not give up, had to keep trying, however long it might take. A spell of really lovely weather encouraged them to move the calf outside onto a high mound of straw where, by stretching only a little, she could nibble grass. At night they lifted her back in case of rain. Sometimes Mary came out to sleep in the steading and sometimes not.

Charlotte had caught the habit of talking to the cows. Brushing away at Chalky's now shining coat she told her it was time to stop malingering. Untruthfully she said, 'You'll be off to the knackers sweetie if you don't get going!' So Chalky did just that. One morning she was out in the sunshine, perched on the mound like a nesting swan.

They saw later how it was done. The two front legs were braced to take the weight of the hind end, and slowly bit by bit and with frequent stops for rest the move was accomplished. Charlotte had treated raw places from the accident with healing ointment and did not want to see wounds reopened, so she bound the back legs with strips from an old sheet. Chalky spent a good deal of time undoing these bandages. Patience was shown by both parties.

During a rainy spell Charlotte and John went to the college for a seminar on 'The Economics of Farming Today'. A leading authority from the university and others were to speak; it would be splendid to hear what they had to say. The professor was a youngish man who spoke in a terse matter-of-fact way and produced facts which seemed to add up to a good deal of sense. While he discussed the problems of large acreages with corn and potatoes grown on a big scale, Charlotte's mind wandered back to Burnside and their own efforts, then focused sharply when she realised he had moved on to stock farms.

'I can tell you,' he was saying, 'the family farmer is no different from the man with thousands of acres. He cannot afford to have any part of his enterprise that is uneconomic or labour-intensive. Particularly must he take his own time into account, record his own hours, write down the cost of this labour and make an assessment of its worth, asking himself the vital question, could my time be put to better use? Above all he must recognise that clinging to an enterprise because his father or his grandfather or his defunct great uncle once found it profitable is out, finished, kaput in today's terms.'

Chalky on her swan's nest drifted into the thoughts of two listeners – hardly an enterprise, but labour-intensive for sure. Both felt uneasy and tried not to meet the eyes of people who knew about the rescue.

The professor was warning: 'Your calving index should be tight, all calves born within a fixed short period. It may mean extra hard work for you in that period but after it you are free to do other work, whatever else you have planned. Any cows failing to calve within your limits – cull them! It sounds ruthless but there is need. Replace dear old Buttercup who sometimes gives a decent calf and sometimes not. You may be content to live on expectation but your banker will not! You cannot afford to be anthropomorphic!' Charlotte almost jumped at the emphasis, stealing a look at the stolid faces of people sitting near. Were they as vague as herself about this word? Her enthusiasm for the professor was waning. John was listening intently, he would have questions in the discussion later.

At home they made for an Encyclopedia:

Anthropomorphism – the attribution of human characteristics to beings above or below humanity in the order of the universe. Plants, animals and even inanimate objects or forces such as stones or the winds are sometimes given human qualities.

'Oh!' said Charlotte. 'I will mention this to

the girls when next I see them!'

After 13 weeks and three days, Chalky was seen to stand shakily on four feet, attempting a step forward before subsiding onto straw in the court. Like the patients in the clinic run by Emil Coué, every day in every way she got better and better. Eventually a bit stunted in growth compared with other calves and dragging her left foot a little, she rejoined the herd.

16

'Ta-erum... Ta-Ta...'

She would after all take the big new chisel, though John would kick up a fuss. She needed a broad, sharp blade to prise muck off the perches. Charlotte looked again at a chisel she guessed John would have given her, one of his old ones, not very wide and the wooden handle all spread out where a hammer had bashed it. It might cause splinters if you used it all day.

And what a day to choose for her on-slaught. Hot, windless, the pink granite of the building sparkling in the sun. The previous owner, adapting the little square pigsty for hens, had fed, watered and collected eggs from them but a thickness of gunge and depth of litter confirmed cleaning their mess had never figured in his routine.

At one time on a day like this she would have lazed in an old peaceful garden, reading, probably falling asleep in the sun. Not any more. Now she was resolute, would attack a job so far left undone partly for the lack of time but mainly because it was so horrible. She suspected, knew, there would be fleas. It made her shudder to think of them left alone to breed in the dark year upon year. It depended on what fleas ate of course, without hens or humans to bite. Gathering up brushes and a spade, she carried them to the doorway and peered inside. It was dark because the window was boarded up and thickly cobwebbed. She wondered if that meant spiders and hoped against hope it did not. She knew nothing about spiders either, and did not want to get close enough to learn. She decided to cover up against anything that crawled, hopped or darted about.

Entering the black hole the first task was to let in light and, as she had seen John do, she prised the wooden boards with the back of a hammer. They did not move at all. After a few more tries she gave up, admitted the old man had been alpha at carpentry in spite of the zero in hygiene.

It was difficult to know how to attack the gunge, it was incredibly hard, resistant even to such a super chisel. It looked as if she would need some sort of a rasp to finish off with – John might have something hidden away. Nesting boxes still held old straw, blackened and solid with the same cement. She poked it out, standing well back as it plopped to the floor. She made the mistake of tackling lower boxes first, so on reaching to the top tier sent debris back into the cleaned ones. It was a labour of Hercules. She did not merely glow as a lady should, but sweated like the long-gone pigs under all the protective layers; her hair drizzled damp and she was scarlet to the roots of it.

The morning wore on. Coming out for air the sunlight dazzled, grass loomed and dipped momentarily. Birds flitted about and there was the hum of bees attending the flowering gold of whins; pebbles in the stream shone pale through softly rippling water. What the hell was she doing in that unspeakable hovel on such a day? She assailed the dried muck with a brutal chisel sending a choking dust into already turbid air and outrage into her head. She felt venomous towards mankind and John in particular. Why should he be enjoying a day off with his cronies? Trickling sweat and unbearable heat obliterated the truth that he had begged her to go with him to the Highland Show and she had refused, saying she could look at cows every day of her life and had no wish to trail along looking at machinery they could not afford. It was to be a surprise for John getting this job done, but why should he get the break when she would be covered all over with bites from everlasting fleas left by a disgusting old man in his beastly hell-hole? She simmered on.

'Excuse me?' The man did not notice how she nearly jumped out of her skin – under an oilskin nothing showed. He did not really see her, was peering into the gloom because he heard scraping and rustling and heavy breathing. 'Mr Grey? Mr Grey? James Seton, Department of Ag–' The introduction faltered as Charlotte emerged blinking into the light. His jaw dropped. He stared, though he did not look like a staring sort, taking in the picture. High summer, a long black oilskin with somebody hidden in it, wellington boots peeping underneath and what might have been a gap at the neck closed by a scarf going round and round. A gloved hand snatching an oilskin hat, a genuine sou'wester, another glove clasping a fearsome chisel, very damaged. The vision stood for long seconds before deciding to speak.

'Ah, Mr Seton, I am Mrs Grey.' The enunciation was very clear, as perfected by nuns long ago. As she extended a hand it was faintly reminiscent of Queen Victoria at Balmoral. She went on politely, 'Is there anything I can do? My husband is not here.' She did not elaborate; her father had been strong on that point, she could almost hear him: 'Never bother to explain Charlotte, when you are caught out. Just leave it.' His eyes, full of humour, would have taken in this situation. 'Why bother? This chap would never get it in a million years, and why should he? The gals he knows do not wear oilskins on a summer day as you do darling idiot!'

Charlotte took another look at Mr James Seton. His mouth was closed now but he was still staring, not quite able to accept her, multi-layered in the glare of the sun. Flushed with embarrassment he had taken off his glasses to wipe them with an immaculate handkerchief. Gleaming white shirt, light grey flannels, his shoes highly polished at odds with the rough road, it had been a struggle for him to touch the hand she offered, streaked with hen-muck, though it was rarish, antique stuff.

Mr James Seton tore his eyes away and retreated to the car she had not heard approach, occupied as she was in a different atmosphere, a choking, thick, rancorous one

166

she was glad to leave for a while. Mr James Seton took up a file from the passenger seat and flipped through it to find the reason for his visit, probably wishing himself safe at home in Gallowgate. He spoke in a rather strangled tone, the accent from one of the islands, Orkney perhaps.

'A fencing matter it is Mrs Grey. Er, application for grant, sent in by Mr Grey. I am not sure, should I come back sometime when he is here?' The thought of leaving very desirable it seemed to this young man.

Somewhere deep inside Charlotte lurked mischief which rarely surfaced in their new surroundings. Certainly it was not inherited from her mother, who had been quiet and rather serious. From her father? Well, perhaps. Mr James Seton was to witness it now, catch a glimpse; she could not resist.

'Mr Seton, I know exactly where the fence is to go. Wait and you shall see!'

She did not mean the new fence only! Before leading him to the proposed site she had to get rid of the sweltering outfit. In her mind she produced a silent replay of 'The Stripper', never included in a convent's musical syllabus. She removed a glove and tossed it to one side, the other glove, after a careful loosening of each finger, flicked after it; the scarf slowly unwound from her neck was allowed to float gently away. She wriggled out of John's oilskin and dropped it casually on the doorstep of the hell-hole; one by one she kicked the welly-boots into touch, all in time to silent music which almost shouted aloud. She stripped the fine inner pair of gloves from hands which she ran through her hair with a beaming triumph, then: 'Follow me!' she said, and set off at a tremendous pace in her thick socks, hearing him labouring after her. It would make a great story for both of them.

She returned to the black hole with a lighter heart and made steady progress until everything was cleanish. Digging out the floor could be left for another day and another burst of energy. It was time to eat but first the luxury of a shower and a close look at her own surfaces for little pink dots. She hummed the tune aloud, shedding things with even more verve this second time. She was going to leave them all outside to freshen and for the night's chill to liquidate anything that moved. She wondered if things that hopped or flew had dared to sully Mr James Seton's modesty. Before going into the farmhouse she hid the chisel.

17

'The necessity for this operation'

To the humanitarian who has not an extens-
ive acquaintance with animals the necessity
for this operation may not be obvious...
Veterinary Dictionary: reasons for castration

Charlotte skimmed over the given reasons
for castration in their well-thumbed farming
'bible', the most important being that bul-
locks and heifers could be housed together
and live together without fighting or becoming dangerous to man. She also, with some
relish, read out to John 'the uncertainty of
the temper of an entire male animal (is) well
known'. John kept an impassive face as he
dialled the vet's number and entered the
arranged date and time into the diary: 'Vet
for castration', later adding an 's'.

Their first encounter with this routine job
was not something John looked forward to
and he was glad Gilbert would be coming to
help. On his friend's advice he waited

through the sultry days of July when flies were everywhere until the present cooler weather at summer's end.

'Calves will be bigger and harder to handle,' he told Charlotte, 'but I prefer that to risking fly-strike, which must be the very devil. I'm willing to take Gil's word and avoid that.'

All farming operations were well-thought out beforehand. As a newcomer this was necessary but John was a natural maker of lists, a 'Be prepared' man. It usually paid dividends. It had to be said that he was pretty nifty also when the unexpected struck.

For this day's work he added a second gate to the hinges of one barring off a bull pen in the steading. One animal at a time pushed through into the pen would naturally move towards the gate and the second gate, rapidly swung and secured, would entrap it.

He explained the idea to Gilbert. 'We'll have a strong rope on the second gate and Charlotte standing outside can bend it swiftly round the bar of gate one. No risk to her and she's always quick. The animal will be in the vee-shape made by the two gates and the rope will stop him backing.'

Gilbert agreed. 'Should be nae problem

John. Ye did well with gates frae the Mony-
musk lad; I reckon these wid tak' care
o'anything; bit ye need guid gates if ye keep
bulls.'

'Maybe it's me again expecting the worst,
Gil? Charley in fighting mood rather than
quiet.'

Charlotte got instructions: she was to
stand outside the pen ready to bend the rope
round the bars of the front gate as soon as
John swung the second one. She had to be
quick, and if there was any rough stuff avoid
getting her hands trapped against the bars or
burned if the rope scorched through them
beyond control. She felt the usual qualms
but said only, 'Sounds easy. Anything for an
encore?' There was no reply because John
and Gilbert were walking away, still planning.

It was decided that mothers and calves
were to be brought into the main court
about one hour before the vet was due; all
outer doors to the steading would then be
closed. Gilbert and John would next separate as many bull calves as they could into a
broad passageway outside the court. Later
Gilbert would syphon them one at a time
through into the bull pen where John would
swing the gate, Charlotte secure it and the

vet perform the deed. That was the theory.

All knew that anything could happen to knock theory on the head – giving a surprise or two was animal nature – so 'softly softly' was the watchword. John was convinced cows always sensed when something was afoot, and took no time at all to be 'agin' whatever it was. He guessed it might be a noisy session. Getting 'victims' out of the court would never be with mums' consent.

Came the day. Gilbert arrived in good time and the herd and followers were easily brought to the steading. Troughs were full of good hay and soon there was hardly a noise except that of jaws rolling in sweet content. Calves joined in if they could get at the hay, others settled on piles of straw. It was too early to make a start so Charlotte suggested coffee, as always ready on the Aga. The smell drifted out to tempt them into saying 'yes'.

Separation went well until one cow under-stood what was going on and started to bellow. Others caught on, and the noise grew, extra hay failing to quell it. About 20 calves were outside the court jostling each other a bit when John decided to call a halt. He had spotted the yellow tags of two heifers, extracted probably because taking them through had secured several bull calves at the same time. When opportunity came they could be moved back.

Inevitably the vet was late. This was accepted because one day your own crisis might cause the delay and somebody else's fractious beasts protest at being inside too long. On the whole the reasons for delay were genuine if you had the right vet. When an ugly Japanese off-road vehicle drove up a man they had not seen before got out. He introduced himself and was ready with poised syringe when the first animal was secured. Seeing Gilbert having a struggle to get the next one through the rather narrow side door, the vet flattened himself against the wall as John did to delude the creature into thinking no one was there. He seemed to adapt quickly to the set-up and their way or working.

Holding onto the rope, Charlotte had an instinctive urge to shut her eyes, blot everything out. Surprisingly docile when trapped, trembling and defeated, the first animal evoked a terrible pity: she caught sight of eyes rolled back showing only the whites. The vet had begun, intent and sure in a routine operation. John by an effort of will must have wiped out all feeling because this awful job had to be done. She tried to do the same, knowing she would never be a real farmer's wife, it asked too much.

As time went on she became so busy that thinking did not come into it. Getting the rope round the bars quicker than the victim could back out was crucial. Few bulls accepted fate like the first; the more powerful older ones plunged and kicked in panic. One with its foreleg splayed through the bars had to be released before the leg snapped. Captured again it reared and almost managed to lever itself out of the trap. They had to call in Gilbert for added weight, the rope shortened dangerously before the vet could work. It was hard to believe this twisting sinewy mass was the doe-eyed gentle creature Charlotte knew, offspring of a favourite cow.

The vet explained exactly what he did: an injection of anaesthetic for the older, heavier calves; then disinfectant applied before slitting the scrotum to remove one testicle and slitting again for the second. These were pulled out rather than severed because a tear heals more quickly than a cut. There was bleeding, but not much. A day or so and the whole thing could be forgotten. 'Bar complications?' John remembered the dire things he had read.

'Hardly ever nowadays,' a reassuring grin. 'Just keep the fingers knotted for a while!'

It came to an end. The castrated ones were shed into an empty court and others extracted to fresh uproar. It was a point in the new vet's favour that he helped instead of taking a breather while John and Gil struggled. Eventually Charlotte opened the big doors of the main court and cows rushed out, taking heifer calves to freedom. The mothers of bull calves lingered miserably, nosing at a few remaining bits of hay, now and again producing a pitiful hoarse sound intended as a roar. The smaller bulls gave little trouble, any resistance was easy to deal with. Teamwork was honed to perfection by the time the gates held the last victim.

In spite of wearing gloves, Charlotte had sore hands from the rope. She had made one bloomer, slackening too soon when she mistook the vet's murmured counting of 'One' for 'Done'. It caused a stir until the poor creature was tightened in again. She managed a quick shower before the men returned from getting all the beasts back to their field. More Brownie points for the new vet taking the trouble to help with that. To her further satisfaction she saw three pairs of stout boots outside the door: stockinged feet would not hurt the white rug. Different vet, better habits!

'Great to have that over and done with!' John took off the clingfilm from a plate of sandwiches while Charlotte poured tea. They were relaxed and easy, knowing things had gone well. Robert Wyatt said he had joined the vet practice six months ago, moving to Scotland when his wife's mother was widowed. They lived in her house with their small daughter but were looking for a house of their own. He had worked in the Yorkshire Dales, supposedly Herriot country, and knew places John and Charlotte mentioned. Gilbert thought he knew the Scottish wife, had probably been at school with her brother. Reluctantly the chat had to stop when a telephone message directed Rob to a farm where they wanted him to look at a calving cow.

Charlotte went to feed her cats and was surprised to find two only; seldom did any of them miss a meal. After clearing things away and washing up she decided to write letters. There was always one to answer and it was a good way to unwind. It was nice to think she need not approach a cow for hours. John was checking the heifers and Charley. She reread the last letter, full of gossip about old friends living the sort of life she used to lead. She wrote the farm address at the top of the page and then stopped; it was getting harder to keep in touch – it was just that their lives were so different. She feared her own letters containing hardly anything except cow talk must be boring beyond words. She began to write, commenting first on her friend's news then gave only a brief account of the day's work. Later there was a postscript:

You will not have forgotten Grey Boy, my cat you coveted, saying he was too beautiful to make a farm cat and would be happier left with you? Well, there is news for you my dear! After the gory operations described above he was missing, did not come in for food like the other two so I went to look for him. Guess what? I can hardly believe this myself – he was in the bull pen where all the manhoods were shed, had sorted them out from straw on the floor and was *eating them!* Not a farm cat? He is back now and disposed very elegantly on his velvet cushion (purple it is), spending time on that great plume of a tail. He has a terribly superior look on his face!
Love, C.

18

'...a very small 2nd-class carriage...'

Against a sky spread with grey-green, pink, violet and gold, snow gleamed faintly from the summit of Lochnagar so the well-being of folk in the Howe was not at risk. Pockets of mist enhanced smells rising from short-cropped grass, from bushes of gorse and broom and trodden earth in front of the steading; drifting warmth from cattle reached the man waiting at an open steading door.

He was a stranger who at first glance might well have stepped from the pages of a racing yarn: bold check jacket, riding breeches, leggings clasped over the calves of slightly bandy legs. A closer look showed the jacket faded, not very clean and the leggings and boots in need of a polish. As there was no horsey enclave in the region it was likely the look was pseudo, chosen to give an impression he admired rather than what he did for a living. He seemed unconscious of the glory in the sky, allowing the sun to go down without remark, his hard little eyes focused on John Grey. When John came forward the man murmured his name which John did not catch.

'Sorry, what name did you say?'

'Gooch, Jim Gooch.' His hand had known hard work, his face too was leathery with an odd greyish look. There was an undertone of apology as he explained the reason for his visit, but none the less his words had a wheedling quality as if no reasonable man could refuse what he asked. John Grey did not feel reasonable.

'I just do not believe what I am hearing Mr Gooch! You say the railway carriage over there belongs to you? You bought it when old Judd had his roup before I moved here nearly two years ago? If that is true, and this is the first I've heard of it, I have to ask why the hell did you not come before or telephone me about it?'

The man fumbled in his top pocket and produced a grubby paper. 'Here mister, fae the auctioneer, the one that selt me et. Ma ticket o' receipt.' Slowly he read: 'Received from Mr J. Gooch, the sum of one hunnerd an' sax poun', an' signed by Aiberdeen an' Northren Marts!' Triumph momentarily lifted his gravelly voice, yet the delay had to be a stumbling block. Wheedling again he said, 'Ye see man, Judd were a sort o' kizzen, een or twa times away ye ken. Onywye 'e said I could leave 'er as long as I winted sae lang as I'd peyed an' I did as I've shewed ye!' He waved the crumpled paper again but when John made no move pressed it back into the place where it had waited for the earth to circle once and almost twice round the sun.

John made another attempt. 'But Judd never mentioned selling it, in fact quite the opposite, I remember him saying it would be useful to me, as a store.' His voice trailed off as the little man interrupted eagerly. 'It wid, jis' so! The very dab! Div ye ken noo fit a'm aboot?'

Astonishment was giving way to a feeling of helplessness against the expectancy in the little gimlet eyes. John wished Charlotte had been there to confirm he was not unfair – two years was a very long time. He made an effort, choosing his words very carefully.

'Mr Gooch, you buy at the roup and think you have permission to leave the coach here, which you do for nearly two years without a word to me, the new owner of the farm. You make no approach, do not telephone me and yet you believe it is there waiting for you to pick up when the spirit moves?' Exasperation was mounting in him as Mr Gooch looked down at his scuffed boots and then sideways into the steading where a few cows lingered, settled for an hour or two on dry straw. Finally his eyes came back to John, stony-faced, waiting.

'Ye ken, I wis fu' at the roup fin a bocht the thing an' didnae fairly min' aboot it, an' whiles I wis thinkin' hoo a wid git it hame.' He paused as if trying to figure out what such a foreign kind of lad would think of what came next. 'An' then, weel a hid a bit o' tribble, a wis gey unlucky ye ken, gien a spell i' the jile, bit a'm oot noo, gaun tae sort masel'.' He cocked his head to one side, ready for the benison of sympathy; yet the eyes probing John's were not hopeful, maybe too many hopes had foundered before this day. Certainly he did not understand when John turned away, wanting suddenly to laugh. It was so rich: it was foolproof! Short of being dead there was no better excuse than being in jankers! Where could it have been, Craiginches? He hoped not Peterhead or Barlinnie. Still, that was none of his business but it did account for the funny complexion and close-lipped speaking. In a way he had seen it before, in Her Majesty's Royal Navy, men guilty of all manner of things, missing the liberty boat back to the ship, fighting in bars in Plymouth or in Pompey, Gibraltar, Malta. 'Causing an affray' might be the charge or something seriously worse. A line of men standing, hats off, at attention. Whether the face was young or older with signs of wear it was the semblance of innocence, the hurt look... 'Gey unlucky', all the captain's defaulters waiting for a plea of mitigation from the 'crusher', or a damning recital of misdemeanours if they were 'skates', 'no-hopers'.

John wrenched his mind back from the system which served the Royal Navy so well. This man Gooch, what sort of offence had landed him in 'brig'? And how long for? It wasn't relevant except for the sham of innocence. He sighed. The sky was darkening, the mists cold enough to make him conscious of an ache between the shoulder blades. He was also hungry. He spoke abruptly and watched the greyish face go sullen.

'I'll have to think about it Mr Gooch. I take it you can wait a day or two more after all this time? Just leave it with me will you?' He held out his hand for the hardened and this time unwilling palm. 'So I will say good evening to you and we'll be in touch, right?' Then politely, 'Take care on the road now, I haven't got round to repairing all the holes yet!' He turned back into the steading and waited, looking at the beasts until he heard the car start up and move off down the road that might or yet might not one day be made into a smoother ride. Absently he pushed a little more hay into the nearest trough and saw Gertie pounce.

'Well, lassie?' he asked, a frown creasing his forehead, 'what do you think of that for a yarn?'

Getting the auctioneer to the telephone took time: after repeated urgent messages John finally spoke to the head man at the mart the morning following the visit from Gooch. There was a long pause after he outlined the problem and as expected the response was not too favourable.

'He had a receipt ye say? Oor receipt? That we can check, though I didn't handle it maself. It's a rum 'un Mr Grey, I must say. A gey time to wait before upliftin' an' ye're usin' it of course? Handy thing for storage, keepin' things dry, cattle nuts, minerals, that sort o' thing.' John realised the man was thinking as he went along having nothing to offer in the way of a solution. 'Detained at her Majesty's pleasure, you say? Weel, she'd nae wait for him to tie any loose ends, he'd be awa' pretty smartish once he was ta'en.'

John sighed. 'There's no time limit then, on somebody removing what they've bought at a roup? You don't say specifically it must be uplifted before such and such a date or else?'

'No sir. Nothing legally binding I fancy. Not that I've heard of such a time gone by as in this case. You could of course query it, but lawyers aye cost money ye might not get back, win or lose. I reckon he'd put up a guid tale, get the aul' biddies on his side in the court, and the whole damn thing recoil, an' still it would be to move, ye ken?'

'Just as I thought myself. My trouble is the damage he might cause shifting it. I'll have another go at him anyway, see if I can buy it back, though he seems set on having it for some reason, maybe because he can see I'm agin it! Anyway thank you for your time.' An exchange of courtesies before each man put down the telephone. John looked out to where leaves drifted onto the shabby roof of the coach, long since devoid of original paint. It would be tricky to move from where it had rested for heaven knows how long.

Charlotte had planted a climber, a quick grower which sprouted heart-shaped leaves camouflaging what might have been an eyesore. She was also encouraging ivy to trail across so eventually all would be hidden. Now, if the coach had to be removed from such an established nest, the vital question was 'How?'

'Charlotte, come and look at the thing.'

She had a smudge of flour on her forehead which disappeared in a furrow of concentration. There simply had to be a way out of this one. 'All that stuff to move out and put somewhere, but there's the easy bit. I'd like to zotz Gooch, maybe give him a whisky laced with something nasty! I can't bear to think of machinery in there dragging it out. I know it's hardly a real lawn but it took so long to get this far. When you think of the wilderness it was, and for the first time we have colour, the beginnings of a garden!' Both thought of the garden in England and could not speak of it. John realised how much effort it had taken to recoup this particular bit of old Judd's legacy.

'Don't worry! I promise you the beggar will move it my way or not at all! Leave it with me!' He seemed always to be saying, 'Leave it with me!' All problems found their way to him: it would be nice to slide out from under, say leave it to somebody else, God perhaps, or the Pope? One thing was clear, the little nut of a man was not going to spoil Charlotte's garden. He began to make plans, going outside to make absolutely sure of the facts, ready for the next visit of laggard uplifter Gooch intent on disturbing their hard-earned peace.

It was a couple of days later when Charlotte saw the old car chugging up the farm road, and as arranged she ran to tell John who was in the empty steading preparing the cows' next feed.

'OK. Now, you disappear and don't bob out with the café-hemlock. Leave it to me!' Once again, he thought, grinning and giving her a 'thumbs up' sign. He waited and then strolled to the close to meet Gooch as he pulled to a halt there.

'Ay ay, fit like Mr Grey? Ye hiv the signs o' a bonny day!' John bade him a civil 'Good morning' but did not waste time discussing the nature of it. There was an anxious pause before the key question.

'Yon coach, ye've thocht it ower Mr Grey? It's squeerly mine as a tell't ye! A'm nae leein' aboot it!'

'That may be so but I am not sure how a

court of law would view it after all this time. It should have been uplifted straight away after the roup as you well know. But say it is yours and you are going to move it I wonder how you propose doing that? What machinery had you in mind?'

'Well, a'm nae sure, a tractor? Wid a hae the loan o'your een? A Zeetor is't? Fowks spik weel o' that machine. We'd easy git it deen wi'the Zeetor.'

'I am sorry but no chance! Quite right it is a good little tractor but it would not shift that coach; isn't man enough; just not up to it!'

A stubborn set to the face, the voice a mite truculent. 'A wid hae thocht...' it was plain he did not believe John. 'Weel if ye're nae willin' tae help a'll jis' set aboot hirin.' A pause and then another tack. 'Yeer neipers, wid onny o' them gie's the loan? Sillert fowk some o' them wad be? Bit a wid allus pey a poun' or twa...'

John spoke. 'I am not asking them, Mr Gooch, and I advise you not to for one good reason: no tractor is going into my garden to drag that coach out!'

A flush spread over his face and he began to bluster. 'I ken jis' fit ye're aboot mister, an' it's nae gaun tae wirk wi' me. Yon coachie's mine. I bocht it an' ye're nae deein' ma oot o't! Bluidy foreeners, all the same kin o' smart erses comin' aboot takkin' the lift.' He was interrupted by a hand lain not too lightly on his shoulder and a face brought close so there was no misunderstanding between them. John spoke calmly and without animus.

'There are two good reasons why I will not have a tractor in my garden, and one of them need not concern you. The main reason is to do with the oil pipe feeding the boiler for my central heating. Now I did not find out until it was too late to do anything about it that the trench dug for the pipe was far too shallow – either the workman was lazy or the ground too hard, I simply do not know. What I do know beyond doubt is that a heavy tractor and a much heavier railway carriage cannot pass over that very shallow trench without fracturing the pipe.' He waved away an interruption. 'I'm sure you would not want to do so but if you fractured the pipe you would be faced with very heavy costs when I got the court to order you to put it right, plus what I should be awarded in damages for being without heating as winter comes on. Need I go on?'

The man was unwilling to give ground. 'I

could mak' sure I didnae brak yir pipe, we cuid somehoo...'

Interruption very firmly from John: 'There's no question Mr Gooch. It's no go. For you or a tractor. Believe me!'

'Weel fit the hell am a suppost t' dee then? Ye canna deny it's mine, thet I bocht it, bit if ye winna lat me in yir bluidy garden...'

John saw his chance. 'This coach you have left for so long, I have begun to wonder, do you really want the trouble of moving it or are you really trying to get your money back? I could well understand if that's what you're after. And if so, what price do you want, have you decided?'

Gooch was tempted, John could almost hear numbers clicking behind the sharp little eyes fixed on him. It could be the tale of London riches surfacing yet again.

'It wid hiv tae be plenty, tae compeensate ye ken, a wid say about a thoosan' or...' Seeing John's expression he said, 'nine hunnerd maybe?' A pause to see if he was on the right track. Once more the man's barefaced cheek made it difficult to keep from laughing. Not bad on the spur of the moment, that sort of profit!

'Forget it Mr Gooch. Let's concentrate on how you are going to get your coach. Have you thought of hiring a crane? And of course you'd need a low-loader. Without damaging the wall a crane would lift and swing the thing over onto a loader here on the road.'

'A crane! A bluidy crane! An' loader!' It was Wimbledon and John McEnroe – 'You caaint be serious!' – and John Grey was the referee who had seen it all before.

'To be honest Mr Gooch I am not very keen on any of it. A crane would not do my field any good. Impact the soil too much. But I recognise there isn't much alternative for you. I take it you don't want to sell to me at any price I would pay?'

He grasped the straw but the idea of profit still lingered at the edge of his mind. 'An fit micht be the price ye wid pey, tae compeensate fae the loss o' ma store an' ma time an a' that?' He waited for an answer he did not like when it came.

'I would pay just what you paid, sir, one hundred and six pounds, maybe make it up to one hundred and ten allowing for inflation. I think you would be lucky at that, getting your money back on it after all this time.'

Rage quite transformed the little man, his greyish pallor replaced by a nasty red suffusing face and neck, blue veins pulsating at his temples as he quivered almost danced at the enormity. 'Ye ... ye bluidy Sassenach! Ye're tryin' te haud on til't yersel! Stealin'! Fowk gets jile fae that! Bit ye'll nae git awa' wi't, I'll git the gear an' a'thing te move the bugger so ye can jis' kiss ma erse Mr Fine Bluidy English!' He stomped off towards the car turning again to have a go: 'Ye've got the wrang een te tangle wi' this time mister. Ye micht weel be sorry! Thirs gweed freens o'mine wha'll nae like seein' me bested, richt bastards some of 'em ye ken, aye gang thir ain gait an'dinna gie a shit! Dee onythin'! Michty roch fowk if thir danders up, nae problem gittin' them to sort ye! So ye'd bitter watch yersel 'n' a'thing. Jis watch oot mister! A'm telling ye, keep lookin' ower yir shouder!'

Protesting noises from the car slammed into gear and launched down the road too fast for its old frame. John finished work in the steading before going inside where Charlotte reproached him.

'I saw you John, take him by the shoulder and push your face at him. Surely there was no need to bully the poor little man.'

John decided not to repeat the whole of the 'poor little man's' message. 'He'll be in touch soon I think,' he said thoughtfully, and reached for the coffee pot.

After the morning mists cleared it seemed the day would have a lot of heat considering the time of year. Charlotte decided to make the most of it as a wash-day, collecting everything left for such a day: curtains, covers, workclothes; it felt good to make an onslaught when household things so often came second on the farm. She pegged out the latest batch from the machine and stood to enjoy the sight of a full clothes line moving in just the right amount of breeze, whilst far below in the Howe the air would be quite still. It was then she saw a car she did not recognise coming up the farm road.

Whoever it was would want to see John and he was away for the day helping Gilbert, something or other to do with sheep. It was a nuisance to be interrupted; she had hoped for a clear day but went in to check that coffee would be ready. People usually accepted a cup; she was inclined to think some reps timed visits around 11 o'clock. No one came to the door, so obviously the people had stopped at the steading looking for John there.

The two men were strangers, walking round the building and taking a pretty good look at the hay and straw and everything else stored inside. They turned when Charlotte approached and answered 'Yes' they did want John. They half-smiled at each other as they spoke, which made her feel slightly uncomfortable. One looked like a heavyweight boxer, very tall and broad-shouldered, with nose askew in a battered face. The other man was taller still and only slightly less bulky. Not the usual thing for most visitors to Burnside, they wore smart suits, pale in colour and fitting rather too tightly against muscular arms and thighs.

Charlotte explained that John was not in. Oddly, because it was untrue and she did not usually tell lies, she gave them to understand he would be back shortly. It was a mistake because after another exchange of glances the men said they would wait. Trying to prevent this she asked, 'Can I help at all? I know most things about the farm.' Smiles again. Apart from the fact of being giants there was something else making her feel uneasy; they were an odd pair. She wished she could get John back home but he would be nowhere near a telephone.

'Can you show us the garden missus, with the railway carriage in it? Our friend Jim Gooch sent us.' Again some amusement between them at a joke she did not share. The accents were not Scottish, more neutral, affected mid-Atlantic, maybe with a trace of Ireland. So it was the Gooch thing once more, she might have guessed. She led the way to the garden, puzzling how to get out of a situation brought about by a stupid lie. She had wanted them to think John would be back any minute simply because she was nervous at being alone on the farm, but there was something odd. Then she squared her shoulders, and her face took on what John called the Grace Darling look. Sometimes you had to stop sheltering behind a man and rely on your own good sense. She was going to play dumb!

She showed the men the coach with the carefully trained planting intended as cover for the eyesore it had been at first. She detailed the cost of shrubs planted, with names both common and Latin if she knew them, appealing disarmingly for help when she did not. She dwelt on what the place had been like before they took over; she insisted on showing exactly where the oil pipe crossed the garden and offered to get a trowel so they could dig and see how shallow the trench was. She embarked on the tale of the men who installed the boiler and how she suspected they short-changed both their boss and John. When she judged they had relapsed into a sort of glassy insensibility she gave her brightest smile and apologised.

'I am so sorry, I know I talk too much; my husband always tells me I do, but it is so nice to meet new people, especially when they show interest. Now why don't you both sit on the seat there and I'll get you some coffee. I can't think what is keeping John.' They appeared quite glad to sit down.

She took trouble setting a tray with fine china and a large pot of coffee. She put it on the seat between them and then asked anxiously if they would have preferred tea. 'Na, na missus, cawfee's just fine, thank you.' The boxer was the spokesman. The other just nodded.

'You must have something to eat with the coffee then. I'll get you some of my home baking!' She smiled again. It was beginning to be a bit of a lark providing she did not overdo it. She tried to remember dear little housewives she had come across. In the kitchen she had freshly baked scones, which she piled on a plate, and from a tin she took the sponge cake intended for John's tea. After a second's thought she split it into three parts, spread jam and cream on the layers, and cut it into enormous slices. Adding a pot of butter for the scones, knives, plates and two crisp napkins she carried the second tray out.

'Shall I butter the scones for you or will you manage?' They were quite eager to manage. 'Well do shout if you need anything more, I shall be in the kitchen, I'd better get some ironing done I think.' She gathered a massive armful of clothes from the line. 'More coffee if you need it!' she trilled returning to a woman's rightful place.

She folded the clothes and stuffed most of them into the airing cupboard. Except for shirts and blouses she hardly every ironed nowadays. After a while she went outside, got the wheelbarrow from the workshop and trundled it back to the garden, placing it just in front of the coach. The men were still eating.

'Don't mind me! You know, woman's work is never done!' She unlocked the coach door and climbed in, emerging seconds later with a bag of cattle food which appeared heavier than it really was. Manoeuvring it into the barrow she set off for the steading where John intended to store all the stuff displaced by nuisance Gooch. She went back for a second sack and noticed Boxer looking uneasy. Returning for a third found him with a sack lifted on his shoulder which he placed carefully in the barrow and then, as if it were a feather, scooped up another to rest athwartships.

'C'marn Mike,' he growled to his friend, 'stir your stumps man, wheel this for the lady.' He took off his jacket and Charlotte looked with admiration at the bulging muscles.

'My, my!' said Scarlett O'Hara before Charlotte could resume her own way of speaking, 'you certainly make very light work of it but there's really no need.' Looking modestly at her hands, which were small but firm and tanned, she continued, 'I can do it, truly, I am used to hard work!'

Mike was getting used to the barrow and relaxed his saturnine features enough to say, 'No bother missus, you sit down, your turn for a rest.' They worked away, now and again stealing a look to make sure she was still impressed by the way the sacks appeared weightless lifted by such arms and the barrow seemed to wheel itself with three or four sacks piled across it. Indeed she was genuinely impressed, she had not expected it from those suits. Nibbling at a piece of sponge she wondered what John would say.

Just as the last load was whisked away she went inside and brought out two generous drams and a small glass of lemonade to keep Scarlett's image intact. They decided not to wait for John. She thanked them profusely for their help and they thanked her for the food, agreeing it was a treat to have home-made stuff nowadays. Boxer's battered face was transformed by a huge beam of a smile as he drove off and Mike had quite a satisfied look on his face. Being so large they must have enjoyed the afternoon and the physical effort with jackets off, rather as enormous dogs kept in small houses must feel when freed from the leash on a real country walk. She cleared up the remains of the snack and went to find something for John's tea.

Giving him an edited version of the visit she said, 'Odd the way things happen, isn't it John? I did not care at all for them at first, yet they proved to be so helpful.'

The dear little housewife fussed to make sure John had sufficient to eat. Scarlett lingered to explain about the helpful men, dwelling too much perhaps on physique and heavy bags made feather-light. Then came a question from Charlotte with a very straight look at her husband: 'Have you some idea

John, what they wanted you for?'

Jim Gooch did not change his mind but stuck to his sworn intention to move the railway carriage. It must be said that he moved it at great cost, requiring a mobile crane, a low-loader and three powerful tractors.

The coach was hoisted into the field without touching the garden wall. It was dragged a short way on the ground which might have damaged the underneath a little, and finally swung onto the low-loader. Before it pulled away down the uneven road two hefty-looking men made sure the hole in the garden was filled in as neatly as possible.

John had taken the precaution of asking one or two of his friends from the tug-of-war team to be present but there was no need. Apart from a snappish Jim Gooch everyone was cheerful and cooperative and all enjoyed the refreshments.

19

'A Winter's Tale'

It was such a change to read books which had nothing to do with farming, books spread on the table in the kitchen so she could browse through and at the same time keep a check on the Aga oven. As John pointed out it was her sort of thing, selecting, deciding how to put information over, diagrams and funny sketches helping to make things clear. She smiled to think of her first reaction, how annoyed she was.

'You are a rat John Grey, an absolute rat! Landing me with it, sliding out from under because you didn't want...'

'It wasn't like that. As usual you're steering the wrong course.' An infuriating grin. 'He asked me and I said I couldn't possibly so he said what about you.'

'And you said "Good idea", she has nothing else to occupy her mind, she'll oblige.'

'Madam, would I ever dare? Now look, all you had to do was refuse same as I did, but seriously it is something you might enjoy, preparing and...' The look on her face might have stopped him saying she would like to stand in front of a lot of men telling them what to do.

The idea had come from farmers at the annual meeting of the local group. Planning courses to be held in the autumn and late winter, they decided to have sessions on farm accounts, income tax and VAT. Paperwork worried people without much time and energy left at the end of a day: they wanted to be told how to swim and not sink in the rising flood of it. Someone asked for help in writing business letters, saying dryly that whenever he wrote a letter he was always confounded by the reply and when he replied to the reply he got another one foxing him completely. He admitted not paying enough attention at the school when he was a loon, but 'trauchled fermers' like him required help. If some sort of secret formula existed, he wanted it, he was getting old and needed his bed at the end of the day. After a few ribald remarks and some applause it was agreed something on letter writing could be included. That was why John had been asked, and had neatly deflected the request Charlotte's way.

Instead of refusing outright, she reluctantly said she would do it but only if no one else could be found. The relief on the face of the course organiser told her exactly how much effort was likely to go into a search. She could almost see 'Mrs Grey' ticked on his list against 'Letter Writing, 19.30 to 21.30 p.m.', as he left to find a victim for another part of the course.

John had been right though, it was a pleasure to sit in the warm kitchen and plan. Simplicity would be the key, nothing high-falutin', just a good practical approach. She burrowed happily through the references. Preparation, preparation, preparation, drilled into them at the convent until it became second nature to some like herself *Gower's Plain Words*, a mine of information; an ancient grammar once her father's with one surprisingly apt chapter; and notes on Tony Busan's television series which she thought first class. She would take something from each one.

Centrally on a sheet of paper she wrote in capital letters, LETTER WRITING, encircling it in red. From this various arrows would lead to points highlighted as important. She had yet to decide exactly what these were. First there was the boring bit, the conventional layout. With a second sheet into the portable she began to type. Surprisingly the details took up a whole page, there was more to say than one would think. It might be a good thing to have copies duplicated to be kept for reference if people wanted. Notes made in class were usually hard to decipher, if anyone ever bothered. Better to have a clear handout; she would see. Several paragraphs needed elaboration, with examples, good and bad. It would be fun to illustrate, large scale, sort of cartoons. It was going to take up a lot of time but now there was the meal to see to. With regret she moved the books and typewriter to one end of the long table and opened the oven door.

Days went by and the shape of the talk became clearer. It was irritating to be called away just when she was solving some tricky point but the farm came first and John did not call her unless he was desperate for another pair of hands. The young stock was now separated and making a din about it. Weaning was hard on everybody, heartbreaking for calves without mother's milk for the first time, for cows yearning to comfort, for John more work feeding animals kept inside. For Charlotte, nagging regret about the way of things on a farm, the changeless necessary things which sometimes revived doubt in herself as the wife of a farmer. She found the noise unbearable and even worse when loud hopeful braying diminished into pained, harsh croaking. Sometimes when John was out of the way she went into the steading and added more hay and extra rations of calf nuts into the troughs; it was comfort-eating such as human-beings resorted to but the effect was brief, merely a respite until the chorus started up again. She suspected John knew of her inroads into the expensive concentrates and was willing to overlook it because of the stress.

Back preparing for the talk she typed definitions given by the *Shorter Oxford English Dictionary*:

'to communicate: to impart information'
'communication: the imparting, conveying or exchange of ideas, knowledge etc., whether by speech, writing or signs.'

She continued: 'You write a letter when you need information (query) or when you give information (reply). You must ask yourself: Will a reader know from my letter precisely what he or she must reply to?' or: 'Is my

204

letter a specific reply to the questions asked?'

She realised this would be more effective as a chart or diagram in the manner of Buzan, with circles and arrows in coloured pencil. More work.

She hoped to get people questioning the well-worn phrases considered correct in business letters. One need not be 'in receipt of a communication' or 'advised' of some fact rather than told. So unnecessary to thank anyone 'in anticipation of your earliest reply', though of course politeness was important. She went back to the first sheet of paper and from the central circle arrowed SIMPLICITY. Another arrow went to USE then others sprouting to SHORT SENTENCES, SIMPLE PUNCTUATION, THE ACTIVE VOICE OF VERBS. A pattern began to emerge: BE CONCISE, EXCLUDE EVERYTHING THAT IS NOT RELEVANT. She encircled the points of emphasis and used different coloured pencils for the arrows. She had learned this from clever Mr Buzan: it would be easy to work from such a plan.

Interruption. A lorry pulling up on the close, the driver thinking he had arrived at Ron Fox's farm, this sometimes happened. She directed him back to the main road and the second turning along. Before going back to the pattern she put potatoes into the oven to bake; the meal was to be easy, cold pressed brisket, a mix of garlic, courgettes, tomatoes and green peppers already cooked and just to reheat, to be followed by cheese and fruit. No pudding, a sacrifice in the cause of letter writing in the Howe.

Back with the plan she wrote and encircled CLARITY and PRECISION and arrowed to the left of the words BE ACCURATE and BE ORDERLY. She pondered over the right-hand side before deciding the most vital thing to stress was choice of words. Things to avoid were wrong facts, those terrible jargon words and phrases and anything at all slapdash. It would be useful sometimes to enclose a diagram or map with a letter, even a photograph. The word MAKE and from it arrowed A CAREFUL CHOICE OF WORDS, and also A PLAN, DIAGRAM, MAP, PHOTOGRAPH. Downside of this countering MAKE she wrote AVOID with a red arrow to her pet hate JARGON WORDS and asterisks **** in red. Annihilation of a few cherished phrases could be included at that point in the talk. It was all falling into place.

The course organiser was willing to duplicate anything and provided beautiful white cardboard for drawings. Charlotte suspected he was so pleased to find her taking the thing seriously he would have copied a list of cows with herd number, age and progeny without questioning why. The drawings were great fun to do, she managed to make them expressive and very apt, cartoon style. When they were finished she was ready.

The course organiser, Willy Graham, also arranged a break for her in the two hour-session when a girl from an Aberdeen office supplies firm would talk on filing systems. She wondered if there would be a cup of coffee, scorning John's suggestion of a hip flask. He was glad to have her back on farm work and said it was great having a slave again. He did remind her about a lecture he once attended: the speaker believed in 'learning through enjoyment' and in spite of the serious nature of his subject had reduced the audience to helpless laughter. So Charlotte primed herself with what she hoped were witty stories to illustrate her points. She found it hard to imagine farmers in the Howe amused enough to roll in the aisles, but was willing to be wrong.

As it turned out the weather proved to be a major obstacle. Snow fell one week before the date of the talk and seemed likely to lie; roads to the north were pretty near impassable. Before then John and Charlotte had gone to the weekly sessions on accounts, confirming they were on the right lines with what they offered the Inland Revenue and the VAT man. John thought it would be rotten if Charlotte's stint was poorly attended. As always she had put heart and soul into it, and worked out a clever and helpful talk. Ironic then if people thought there couldn't be much of interest and stayed at home because of bad weather. Unfortunately the venue was at the northern edge of the Howe, a village primary school with a pub just across the road, a natural place to wait, John supposed. Charlotte did not want him listening, it would 'put her off' she said. He allowed himself the hope of a generous fire to sit by whilst he drank a lemonade, or something.

The Land Rover made easy work of the journey. John drove and Charlotte huddled beside him clutching her notes. Charts and handouts were in cardboard boxes in the back, more of the latter than needed under the circumstances. It was very very cold. Her gloved hands were numb. The heater in the Land Rover had too much icy metal to combat but if it did not get into full blast soon she believed her teeth would chatter and never stop. The road was deserted. Obviously people had too much sense to venture out. What would she do if no one at all turned up? Get rough she decided, hurl abuse at the organiser for conning her into the thing, maybe hit him over the head with her file. If he was there. The handouts could be thrown into the fire. Oh please God, let there be one.

There wasn't. Seven or eight people were in the classroom wearing outdoor coats, gloves, woolly scarves and caps, shuffling their feet and keeping their hands inside their pockets, except for one or two testing an old-fashioned radiator giving out much less heat than it was capable of. The caretaker of the school, it was decided, had the soul of a skinflint. He was obviously a lickspittle currying favour with the education authority, a crook selling coal on the side, or he just hated farmers. They were never to prove any of this. After a few more braves arrived, Charlotte agreed to begin. It was only fair, she said, before hypothermia set in. She really envied John across the road.

The organiser introduced her quite formally after all the chat about Mr Scrooge, the Janitor, and thanked her for volunteering for a task which he knew had taken up a good deal of time. Volunteering! No thunderbolt fell from Heaven upon his short-cropped head but there was something...

As is often the case in a classroom situation people were reluctant to sit at the front. They left space between themselves and the speaker. Charlotte smiled and beckoned.

'Come close,' she said, 'it could be warmer!' The organiser took the lead, dragging from the back a very small chair – this was after all a room equipped for little children, but the chair was not for the likes of him and could not cope at all. With a violent crack the legs splayed and left only the wee seat pinioned under an ample rear. He was given a lot of advice about slimming and Charlotte got off to a good-humoured start.

The preparation paid off: the handouts saved time and it was easy going through them to emphasise the important bits. People sat foursquare on the scuffed little chairs and listened. No feedback, nobody questioned, disagreed or argued. A couple of men were farmers she knew and some of the women had attended the other classes. Two young men could have been student sons of farmers. There was a very pretty girl and her friend, not so good-looking but with a kindness in her face implying, 'You interest me. Keep going', which was nice.

'Learn through enjoyment' – how true it was. They were thawing, appreciating the carefully thought-out examples. A place now for the old chestnut about the pedantic professor: 'Remember, choose your words carefully? Well, a professor of English at St Andrews was caught by his wife with a beautiful young woman in very compromising circumstances, in the act as it were or *in flagrante delicto* I believe they call it. Naturally she was very upset and reproached him bitterly: "I was so surprised," she wept. "No dear," an automatic correction from the professor, "I was surprised, you were astonished!"'

It might be worth checking in the dictionary if you have any doubt, she said when the laughter subsided. It was an appropriate time for the girl with the files and office gadgets. Charlotte found the pub wasn't too warm either. She asked John if mine host was the caretaker's brother, and said 'Never mind' when he asked what she was talking about. He seemed to have made do with a few glasses of inner warmth so she tossed off a small brandy to keep in touch. She was not displeased with the evening; no one seemed bored to death, as yet, she thought, crossing her fingers and wishing she could keep gloves on.

Quietly she entered the classroom. The talk was finished and the girl was gathering up the office paraphernalia, looking from under a cloud of dark hair to acknowledge Charlotte. With evident relief she said, 'Thank you for listening and now I will hand you back to Mrs Grey and the letters.'

Charlotte thanked her politely and walked to the front. A little buzz of conversation allowed a minute or two to arrange her notes. She felt a warm glow hearing 'Guid!' and some clapping from the back row as she took up duplicated sheets to hand out. The warmth chilled at a hoarse but penetrating whisper 'I cannae wyte fe mair o' the sexy stories!'

Trying to make herself heard over the diesel engine's thump-thump as John drove carefully home on the icy road she explained the quieter second half. 'I thought I'd better miss out a few bits as they obviously misunderstood some of my jokes. Well, some-body did! I kept stealing a look to see who it was but I couldn't tell. They all looked the same, on the back row, sort of expectant. The farmers sat there. I know it was one of them!'

'It would be!' said John, giving her a lop-sided, slightly tipsy look. 'We're a funny lot!'

20

'Millionaire'

One evening late in the year John Grey put his tractor under cover and went inside the steading. A lot of thought had gone into the design of it and more money than he could afford, but the result was highly satisfying. Criticism came to his ears about its stark outline against the dour greens and browns of the Scottish hills: 'Yon muckle court stauns oot,' was an opinion, 'like a sair thoum!' Mildly he had said, 'Wait and see how it weathers.' A good shelter for the beasts was his concern at the time.

The cows ranged tight at wide concreted troughs feeding with a concentration which always amazed and pleased him. 'It is like being in church,' his wife remarked of this intensity, hearing the soft sounds rising to the vaulted roof. Hay and straw and mineral powders were stacked high on a central passage between the cattle courts with enough space left on either side for feed to be handled. Also this was the place for walking round to count or check the beasts, though Charlotte and John sometimes leaned against the stout separating barriers just to look at them and marvel at finding themselves responsible for so many creatures. Farming was said to figure high in the list of dream occupations of men who served in Her Majesty's Navy, perhaps there was a yearning to feel solid earth beneath the feet? John Grey still could hardly believe it was his reality, that he owned a bit of Scotland and a lot of cows. Technically a farmer but without illusion, there was so much to learn.

His cows were similar in age and breeding, at first alike as peas in a pod; then differences became obvious, a block of colour round the left or right eye or both, a face mottled white, a wide streak along the spine, flashes on the feet. They had numbered eartags but it was natural to give them names, not randomly but because some similarity emerged, some characteristic to bring this or that person to mind. A big red and white animal, established leader of the herd was easily Gertrude, a bossy lady they had known; a sweet-natured cow with a soft fringe of hair was Lucy, a friend of Charlotte's. The few told of the accolade said

'Oh!' and 'Really?' unsure of it. They knew John was mad, as the neighbours did: 'Crazy! Kens nocht aboot fermin' an' spends a fortun' on a muckle shed!' 'Wrang in the heid!'

Seeing mouths reaching for hay because turnips always disappeared at great speed and with enormous relish, John came to the same conclusion as his wife: they pray for everlasting turnips in this church, he reckoned. Taking a last look he spoke aloud. 'That's it, girls!' It never felt ridiculous to talk to them and it amused him to search their mild eyes for a gleam of response. 'Everyone's gotta eat. My turn now!' he informed the watchful 'girls' nearest the door, and left the steading.

Better for man and beast inside there he thought, huddling into his coat against wind gusting straight from Lochnagar. The new steading was the heart of the farm. He loved the mixture it offered, from hay something of summer, the cows breathing it out; their warmth; the dryness of straw; fresh dung, not offensive at all; a faint antiseptic from mineral powder. But there were things he had not got right.

He forced a purposeful stride towards the farmhouse where light beamed from every room and powerfully from halogen lamps intended to illuminate the whole of the farm close in an emergency, and only then. It was Charlotte's idea of a welcome home after the sheer hard slog of his day, but it was an extravagance which must stop, she would have to see that.

It began one evening when they came back late from shopping in Aberdeen 30 miles away. He had driven slowly on the rough farm road back to a silent dark house and dusky courts where cattle waited to be fed.

'A house on a hill should blaze with light,' Charlotte decided then. 'Like a beacon, a beacon of hope in a wicked world!' she ended, laughing but with a determination he recognised. He had not said anything but gloomily pictured the happiness of Hydro-Electric at the great surge.

The need for economy weighed heavily on him now and the tale of his riches seemed less of a joke. His money was draining away at a rate of knots with nothing coming in. They had to survive until it did and there was no room for the fantasy of light. But he would tell her gently, and not tonight. It was his birthday. Little had been said before he left at first light for the far boundary of the farm: animals belonging to a neighbour were clever at poaching his grass, slackening old wires by leaning on weak fence posts and then stepping daintily over to complete the trespass. He had worked solidly, digging deep holes for new posts, bracing them up, replacing the wire and clearing away the old stuff. He had eaten sandwiches and fruit, a memory now, and supper was on his mind; he felt sure Charlotte would cook something special. He groaned when it came to him that she might also have spent money on a present.

Their back door opened into a narrow lobby and then a hall adapted as a laundry with washing and drying machines, an ironer on a stand and two deep porcelain sinks. An old-fashioned larder leading from it had made a roomy shower. Charlotte planned the changes suggesting the best way to combat farm mud and worse was to curb it at the door, not allow it past a certain point, all inner rooms kept free from threat. She was right of course but sometimes the price of civilisation was too high: tonight to go into the kitchen as he was, slump into a chair and hold out a mucky hand for a whisky, that would be luxury.

He hung his waxed coat against a wall

covered by gloss paint, probably a bargain buy long ago as it was used on every wall in the house. Unfortunate that Charlotte set about it fiercely, scouring and scrubbing only to find the grime had been much easier on the eye than a bilious green shine. One day John vowed, he would decorate the house, make things nicer for Charlotte the way they used to be in the old house which had been different in every way. When funds were in, whenever that would be.

He stripped and stood under the shower, letting hot water course down his spine to reach the core of his tiredness. He was accustomed now to the hard physical work but there seemed to be a permanent ache in him, a protest from bone and sinew though he had been considered a fit man. He noticed his hands were becoming calloused and a bit ingrained but did not scrub at them. 'Water-sweet' only, he thought, no point in a shine. He dressed in the clean clothes put ready for him and added an old warm sweater. He would have preferred whisky to the wine Charlotte was likely to offer. At the end of this first day of the 44th year of his life he did not care to think how old he felt but it was certainly a helluva lot more than that.

The Aga, though grossly expensive, made the kitchen warm and pleasant, the food in its oven sending delicious signals to his yearning insides. He saw the best china, glass and silver on the fine old table from their other life and registered that Charlotte looked very nice but was smiling oddly. Then he saw what had been done to the walls.

Incredibly, hardly any bilious green was visible: from skirting to ceiling animals were sketched, balloons issuing from them to say 'HAPPY BIRTHDAY'. Cows with smiles and flirtatious long-lashed eyes cavorted more happily than any in cave drawings and were named, sweet Lucy accurately coloured, the most prominent. A black bull stood four-square bearing the label 'St Charley', but warned 'WATCH OOT BIRTHDAY BOY!' A flock of curly ewes slanted marble eyes to 'Boris', a ram, and from their tight little mouths wavering lines led to the message 'SAFELY GRAZE'. From a puddle she had been unable to contain his young sheepdog splashed 'LOVE, LOVE, OOPS, SORRY!' Geese stretched long white necks and orange bills gabbled 'AAH, AAHL BESSST'. Hens clucked and little chicks cheeped. Cats in the process of catching mice turned aside to wish him well; their unfortunate victims expiring managed 'HAPPY BIRTHD–, HAPPY B–', or tragically just 'Hhhh–' An old cat asleep in a basket snored a zig-zag of 'KIND THOUGHTS', oblivious of skylarks overhead. The spaces between sketches were filled by turnips, smiling-faced ones with a flutter of leaves atop. 'SWEDE DREAMS!' they chorused.

John Grey began to laugh as he had not laughed for a long time, weariness lifting from him. 'You are one crazy woman!' he told Charlotte, taking the crystal glass of malt whisky from her hand. A slice of pâté on the plate in front of him smelled good, better than anything the supermarkets could offer. He started laughing again after a first sip of golden liquid glowed in his throat and the sketches offered more and more when he could look a second time and a third. A thought made him splutter, 'How could you? How could you cover up that, that, beyootiful paint?'

Before he went to sleep that night John recalled the day when he and Charlotte first saw the farm, its small fields and crumbling drystone walls. They had made their way to a high point, crossing a stream with primroses clustering on its bank and yellow scented musk spilling into the water; moorhens were gliding on a pool where weed had choked the downward flow. At the top they sat taking it in, the whole farm spread out, dividing walls, the little grey house, tumbledown buildings ... all caught as in a bowl of sunlight among hills which seemed to roll into infinity. The air was cold and the clearest he had ever breathed.

Walking down they had disturbed a flock of tiny birds and heard the soft beat of many wings skimming low at first, then up and up into a cloudless sky. Charlotte remembered that.

It was almost Christmas before there was time to clean off the birthday walls, but the bold strokes from felt pens were not easily sponged away. There remained a haze of what had gone before to puzzle people who saw it, causing them to lose the thread of talk whilst they took a furtive look. Like cave paintings again, things came into focus only after prolonged staring. The mysterious outlines, clouded and vague though they were, did little to cancel the idea of John Grey's eccentricity, or his wife's. Odd, baith the twa o'them, gi'en up the high life for fermin'...

The publishers hope that this book has given you enjoyable reading. Large Print Books are especially designed to be as easy to see and hold as possible. If you wish a complete list of our books please ask at your local library or write directly to:

Dales Large Print Books
Magna House, Long Preston,
Skipton, North Yorkshire.
BD23 4ND

This Large Print Book, for people
who cannot read normal print,
is published under the auspices of

THE ULVERSCROFT FOUNDATION